Triptych of Souls

a novel by
Lezli A. Polm

Copyright © 2014 Lezli A. Polm
All rights reserved.

ISBN: 0692301895
ISBN 13: 9780692301890

Dedications and Acknowledgements

This book is dedicated to my family and dear friends. Without their love and support this book could not have been written.

I owe special thanks to the following people for their creativity, advice, editing skills and above all friendship: Karla Cheselka, Denise Agnew, Donna Amalong and Ashleen O'Gaea of PENtagram Consulting.

Prologue

Destiny is free will, and fate is Karma.

August 1891

The story of Emeline Evans
from *Tales on the Trail,*
a collection of historical folktales
by T.L. Lowery

E meline cleared away the supper dishes, scraping the leftovers into a dish for the chickens. Three-year-old Ivy stood at her side, clutching her favorite rag doll. Covering the table with an oilcloth and a couple of large knitted hot pads, Emeline lifted a steel washtub onto the surface and walked over to the fireplace. A hefty kettle of water hung over the hot coals.

"Stand over there by the door for a moment, Ivy. I am going to fill the tub, and the water is very hot."

"Yes Momma." Ivy moped over to the door. She waited impatiently, hoping to go outside before it started to rain.

Emeline retrieved her thick gloves from the fireplace mantle. She pulled them on, and carefully removed the kettle by its handle. Hefting it over to the table, she set it on one of the pads. She poured the water slowly into the tub, and then placed the steaming kettle on the other hot pad.

"I am going to wash these dishes. After I finish, we will go outside for a bit." Emeline peered out the small window looking east. "By the looks of it, there is quite a storm brewing, so I am afraid there will not be much time for play."

"Hurry, Momma," Ivy pleaded.

Pulling a bar of lye soap and a small brush from her skirt pocket Emeline began scrubbing the dishes in the washtub. She dipped them into the kettle to rinse them, afterward drying them with a linen dishtowel embroidered with roses around its edge. She stacked them aside.

"Ma…ma." The little girl still stood by the door shuffling her feet, looking forlorn.

"All right, you may go out -- but stay in the side yard. I will be there presently."

Ivy's face lit up. "Yes Momma." She turned the knob and opened the door, grinning back at her mother.

Once outside Ivy began to pretend she was giving her doll Victoria a bath. She laid hold of an old milking pail from under the porch. Using it as a miniature bathtub, she imagined a baby splashing in soapy water. The family's real bathtub was located out behind the house. The clothesline ran the length of the house, and Emeline would hang an old quilt over the line to provide privacy when a member of the family was bathing.

As she played, Ivy heard thunder, and saw lightning over the mountains. She was afraid of both, the loud booms and the streaks of light. Maybe, she thought, she should go back inside. At that moment she heard the familiar sound of her father's ax as he chopped firewood down by the creek.

The child loved her daddy with all her heart. He made her all sorts of toys, and brought her sweets every time he made the trek into town. Best of all, he showered her with affection. *Momma might not be too angry if I go down to see Daddy.* She would be safe with him. He would protect her.

So Ivy took the milk pail, turned it over, and placed it next to the gate. She tucked her doll under her arm and stood on the tin bucket. Standing on her toes, she could just reach the latch. Carefully, she lifted it; next, she pushed the gate open just enough for her to slip through. If she opened it all the way, the squeaky hinges would give her away.

Scampering down the path toward the creek, the girl hummed a tune, one that her daddy had taught her. She couldn't remember all of the words, just the part about spinning, singing, and merrily ringing.

Down by the creek, Jonathan was busy collecting twigs for kindling, as well as chopping some small branches from a fallen oak. He leaned his ax against a stump and shoved the logs into a large gunnysack that lay on the ground at his feet. The sky was darkening as the black clouds moved down from the mountains, hovering over the valley below. It was commencing to sprinkle, so he needed to move quickly. Ivy came running as soon as she spotted him.

"Daddy" she squealed.

Jonathan grinned. He stooped lower to catch the child up in his arms. "Ivy, I see that you and Victoria have come to help, but where is your mother?"

"She's cleanin' up the dishes."

"Well, little lady, I doubt she allowed you to leave the house alone."

Ivy was now looking into his eyes with such innocence that he couldn't muster any anger toward her. With her large blue-violet eyes, her mother's eyes, along with her tangle of blond curls, she was no less than cherubic. Jonathan never thought he could love anyone as much as he loved his darling Emeline, yet when Ivy came along, he found himself smitten. He loved her with the same intensity only in a different way.

"We need to get back to the house before we get caught in a downpour"

Jonathan began to gather the last of the cut wood into his sack. Months ago, he had fashioned a strap for the bag so that he could carry it across his chest, leaving his hands free. He now picked up the bag from the ground and lifted it over his head. It was heavy with firewood.

While Jonathan scrambled to protect his ax against the coming rain, Ivy wandered about fifty feet away to the edge of the creek. It was running at a steady clip. She bent down to see if she had a reflection even in such fast water. She held her doll out to have a look, too.

When Jonathan had the ax in the bag with the wood, he called to her. "Ivy, come here. We must get back to the house now."

His voice was drowned out by the sound of a loud thunderclap which precipitated a deluge of rain. Within seconds, he was soaked. Most likely every-thing in the gunny sack would be wet. Frustrated, Jonathan, made for the creek where his daughter now stood, her head down, her hands clutching the doll to her chest.

As Emeline scrubbed, she could hear Ivy as she played in the side yard. The child was such a blessing. She and Jonathan could not have wished for more. Ivy was beautiful, smart. Furthermore, even at the tender age of three, she had a lively sense of humor. Emeline doted on the girl almost as much as her father did.

Emeline jumped when the thunder clapped. It was so close! Without delay, the rain began to fall, coming down hard. She rushed to the door, opened it, and was instantly doused. She shouted. "Ivy, come inside this minute!"

As she stepped out into the muddy side yard, she didn't see the girl. The gate stood open. The milk pail told the tale. Emeline ran through the gate and down the hill yelling Ivy's name, looking through the rain into the tree line on either side of the path that led to the creek. She was sure that Ivy had gone to meet Jonathan; she knew the spot where he would be collecting firewood. They had discussed it just before Jonathan left to go there.

As Ivy stood on the sodden bank of the creek, she began to slide. The ground was giving way underneath her. As she failed to keep her footing, she felt Victoria slip from her hands, and fall into the rushing water. Jonathan was just a few feet away from her when the tot slipped into the water following her doll.

The current snatched her up and swept her downstream in seconds. Her tiny hands reached for the sky in a plea for help.

Jonathan was in the water before he could think. The bag around his neck was an anchor. He went into the cascading flood, frantically trying to free himself from the strap. The current raced him toward his little girl, but he couldn't get loose of the sack. He was losing strength, gasping as he was sucked under the water time and time again.

Horrified, Emeline watched Jonathan struggling, his arms flailing as he fought the current. As she watched helplessly he was swept downstream. Ivy was nowhere to be seen. Crying and screaming, Emeline ran down the side of the creek toward Jonathan stumbling over loose rocks and debris. She called out their names "Jonathan! Ivy!"

Jonathan quickly vanished from the desperate woman's sight. Soaking wet, up to her shins in mud, she wouldn't allow the rain or the lightning to deter her. She searched the creek side and the surrounding forest for Ivy. Emeline's cries rivaled the booming thunder as all around her it crashed. Throughout the night, she followed the creek as it ran east to west.

The forest had given way to flat grassland, and the creek widened its path. The water flowed at a lazy pace as though the last night's torrent had never happened. Exhausted, Emeline sat down to catch her breath. She had walked miles and found nothing. Morning brought her no peace. She was empty. Even her tears seemed to have dried up. She folded her legs up under her chin, resting her head on her knees. She dozed.

She woke with a start when she heard a whistle. Rising, she looked for the source of the sound. Riding toward her were two men on horseback. She recognized them as their only neighbors, Mr. Eastwood and his teenage son Andrew. There were tied up bundles draped across the horses behind the riders. The bodies had been found.

Chapter One

The past may be obdurate and immalleable; however the legends and folktales that emerge from it are as changeable as the humans who tell them. There is always more to the story....

August 2011

Holly removed yet another article of clothing. She had shed her button-down cotton shirt midway through her hike. This time it was her khaki slacks that had to go. She sat down on a large rock, removed her hiking boots and slid her pants off, tossing them into her backpack. Thirsty, she picked up her water bottle.

The sunlight in southeastern Arizona is always warm, but with the increase in humidity on this late August day, the heat felt almost unbearable. She sat now on the crest of the hill wearing a pair of Spandex shorts and a white tank top. Immediately she felt cooler as the slight breeze coming down from the hills behind her evaporated the sweat on her skin. Honey brown strands of hair fell loosely about her face. She reached up to re-tie her hair, pulling it into a ponytail. Her scalp felt tender. She regretted having left her hat in the truck that morning.

Holly decided to take a short snack break before leaving the area that she had grown to love. She pulled out a large red apple and took a big bite of the crisp juicy fruit. This was her last day as a summer intern with the Forest

Service. The following day she would be returning to Flagstaff to complete her last year at Northern Arizona University.

She closed her eyes and relaxed. Absent-mindedly she fingered the brass locket that hung around her neck. She smiled as she listened to the distant sounds of the birds calling back and forth as well as the faint rustle of the oak leaves. The hum of a hummingbird's wings sounded loud in the almost silence.

Looking back to the events of the last three months, she felt as though the summer had flown by. Her last night here, how could that be? She reminisced about her first night in this beautiful high desert. As that first day had come to a close, it seemed that an unseen artist had painted with soft strokes a crimson cloak for the descending sun. *Arizona sunsets just can't be beat.* She had been sitting outside under an elm tree next to her small rental trailer, listening to the birds as they chattered their evening lullaby. A harsh sound 'cree-aak cree-aak' had set her heart racing. Her mind equated the noise to the creaking of old floorboards or worn hinges like those in spooky movies about haunted houses.

Timidly rising, she had moved out from under the limbs of the tree, as she did, she realized that the cacophony of creepy sound was coming from an abandoned windmill. It stood in the fading twilight like a giant, spider arms outstretched moving slowly as the light breeze wafted through the air. A rustling of leaves accompanied the groan of the old windmill. She had taken a deep breath as the tension released. She felt a bit foolish, being spooked by such a silly looking old thing. As she recalled that night, she smiled.

Her musing was interrupted by the sound of her phone's ringtone. Holly set the apple down, furiously digging through her backpack hoping to find her cell before it went to her voicemail.

She muttered, "Why does this phone always fall to the bottom?" Finding it, she grasped it and quickly pushed the answer icon. "Hello?"

Her answer was dead air.

Holly wasn't surprised. Cellular service near the mountains was sporadic. She saw from the caller ID that the call was from her best friend and college roommate, Cassie. Within seconds, the phone rang again.

"Hi Cass."

"Hi girl, what's up?"

"I just finished my last day at the ranch. I'm really going to miss this place, but with all of the digging we've been doing I feel like I'm majoring in archeology instead of forestry."

"I'm glad you'll be back tomorrow night. I've missed your cooking. I don't think I've set foot in a grocery store since you left." Cassie laughed.

This was an ongoing joke between them since it was Cassie with the cooking skills. She was a business major intent on opening her own restaurant one day.

"There's that great new pizza place I told you about. We'll go there to celebrate. I'll even treat you. I go there so often they know my name, and there's this super cute chick that works there."

Holly burst out laughing. "She must be really hot for you to offer to pay."

"Hey, I'm not that cheap!"

"Yes, you are. But seriously, are you calling for something special or do you just miss the sound of my voice? I mean, it's only been like twenty-four hours since we talked."

"Actually, I had a bad dream last night. In the dream, I was watching this scary disaster movie in which one of the characters was you. It didn't end well for her, I mean you. Oh, you know what I mean. When I woke up this morning I realized that Mercury has entered retrograde. So, I'd be extra careful if I were you."

Holly shook her head as she giggled. "Oh, you Witches living by your silly omens."

"You laugh now, but my 'silly omens' have saved your ass more than once. Remember that fraternity party we went to freshman year? We would have been arrested with everyone else, if not for my Witchy senses. Then there was the time –"

"Point taken. But you're not always right."

A sudden rumble of thunder caused Holly to look over her shoulder. Ominous dark clouds were building in the east above the Chiricahua Mountains.

"Cass, sorry to cut this short but there's a storm coming, I have to get moving."

"Be careful." Cassie started to continue with a laundry list of cautionary advice, but Holly stopped her mid-sentence.

"Yeah, yeah, yeah."

Holly grumbled under her breath as she stuck the phone in an outside pocket of her backpack. She pulled her hiking boots back on. *Witches ....Wiccan roommates.... Psychic know-it-alls.... I can look out for myself. I know this area and the dangers. Hell, I'm the one who's been here all summer. I know she means well, but this mothering shit has to stop. It's been four years since Mom and Dad died. I'm okay now, so she needs to stop smothering me.*

Holly secretly wondered if she would ever get past the death of her parents. The accident happened the summer between her junior and senior year of high school. Occasionally she still had nightmares about that day. The morning of the accident her parents had left together to go to work as usual. Normally she would have been with them. They routinely rode together since her school was on the way to their office building. Her parents both worked in offices at the Federal Building downtown. Her father was an attorney and her mother a court reporter. Holly had decided to ride with a friend that day. Even though she knew that decision had somehow saved her life, she couldn't help but feel guilty, ashamed that she was not with them that day. Survivor guilt, that was what her counselor had called it. That first year she lived in a haze, she somehow lost months, swallowed up in her grief. When she finally managed to return to school, another wave of anguish awaited her.

There they had been; students, and teachers, their eyes on her. Heads nodded in her direction as she passed them in the hallways. Fingers pointed not-so subtly as they indicated her presence to their friends. Some were genuinely empathetic but most had never experienced anything like what she was going through. Their responses were a typically human mix of pity, guilt and curiosity that overcome people when they are met with another's misfortune. Most people didn't know exactly how to react or what to say. Cassie had been Holly's savior at school. They didn't share all of the same classes, but at lunch and when they were together, Cassie had a way of breaking the tension and redirecting the conversation to make things more bearable for Holly.

The guidance counselor and the private therapist that Cassie's parents found for Holly helped her through her darkest days. There were many days when she didn't feel like getting out of bed. There were also days when she didn't really want to exist. On those days Cassie's mother was the one who sat at her bedside and coaxed her back to life. Holly might never be the carefree girl she had been before the loss of her parents. She knew she would have to find a strength that she never knew she had.

A rougher, tougher Holly emerged from the ashes. She became bolder. Her attitude could be sardonic. She began using harsher language. Cassie worried that Holly was hiding behind this abrasive façade in order to keep people at a distance. Holly had to admit that Cassie was right. The only other person that Holly had connected with after the tragedy had been a boy named Kevin whom she had a brief romance with. She had needed comforting and he had been there for her.

Time was helping her to find herself again. She had been working on her attitude. Every day was a new challenge and she was making good progress. It was still very hard for her to accept kindness without it feeling like pity and if Cassie coddled, it turned her mood sour. "Don't brood" she told herself out loud.

She rushed to get going ahead of the advancing storm. She capped her water bottle, shoving it and the partially eaten apple into her backpack. Rising, she took a deep breath, stretched and brushed the dust from her shorts. She scanned the area looking for her little red pick-up. Spotting it just beyond the dry creek bed about a mile away, she headed for it at a trot.

The sky began to darken as the clouds rolled in above her. Several flashes of lightning in rapid succession encouraged her to pick up her pace. It always amazed her how quickly the desert monsoon rains descended on the valley.

As she crossed the creek-bed a cloud of dust flew up into her face. She was buffeted from all sides as she found herself in the middle of a dust devil. She squinted as she ran the last few yards to the safety of her truck.

Holly hoisted her backpack off as she rummaged for her keys. Locating her keychain, she pushed the unlock button. She pulled the handle on the door of the truck. At first it didn't budge.

"Open, damn it," she growled. She tried once again with all her might and the door flew open. She staggered backward, almost losing her footing. Regaining her balance, she crawled into the driver's seat, slammed the door behind her and let out a sigh of relief.

As the dust devil began to clear, Holly started the truck's engine and did a U-turn out onto the dirt road. The wind tugged and pulled at the truck as she made the descent toward Turkey Creek Road. Great drops of rain began to create muddy rivulets on the windshield, obscuring her view.

Holly flipped on the wipers as well as the defogger, and then settled in for the ride. She realized that this was the last time she would be making this drive. By next year, she could be stationed anywhere in the States, assuming she was hired by the Forest Service.

The steady beat of the wiper blades soon lulled her into a daydream state. Her mind drifted back as she began to recall her experiences that summer. When she arrived back in June, she had been one of three interns assigned to the Chiricahua Mountains in Region Three.

Brandon and Travis were back at school now, having left a week ago. One of the tasks assigned to the interns had been the cleanup, excavation and cataloging of the Hideaway Ranch. The property had been recently acquired by the Forest Service as a conservation land trust when a distant relative of the original homesteader died.

The ranch comprised one hundred thirty acres of land, including rolling hills dotted with scrub oak and mesquite, grassy meadows that were once used for grazing cattle, a creek which fed a large pond, and several acres of woodland. The only structures that remained on the property were two small sheds, in addition to the old main house.

The house was little more than a stone cabin, in front of which stood a broken down hitching post and some scattered fence posts. Behind the house, on a small hill, was a makeshift cemetery. Three graves, marked by stone cairns topped with small wooden crosses, lay within a boundary of rosemary bushes. Some distance from the house was a pile of rubble, the remnants of what was once a pole barn.

Thinking about the ranch, Holly remembered the day she first saw the homestead. Brandon and Travis had arrived a week before her and were anxious to show her the property. On the hike up to the site, the guys gave a description of the ranch, but nothing could prepare her for the mix of wonder and sadness she felt when standing amid the ruins of the old house.

While she walked through the living room, she paused as a feeling of déjà-vu overwhelmed her. She suddenly knew what the cabin had looked like when it had been a home. The aroma of a savory stew teased her nostrils. Moreover as she turned toward the fireplace, she thought she caught a glimpse of a woman in a long black dress crouched in front of the hearth. That experience should have totally freaked her out, but oddly enough, she didn't feel frightened, just somewhat melancholy.

Upon leaving the ranch that day, they took a route through the tall pines that bordered the east side of the property. The trodden-down path had obviously been used by various hikers over the years. Where the trail crossed the dry creek bed the three of them decided to have their lunch.

Holly excused herself to answer a call of nature behind some brush just beyond the edge of the wash. Walking back, she kept her eyes to the ground. Being a bit of a rock hound, she knew that this area was rich in quartz, volcanic rock, and other minerals. Something shiny glittered in the sunlight. A nice specimen of pyrite lay wedged under a small shrub.

Digging for the rock, she spied what appeared to be a necklace. The chain had wrapped itself around the base of the bush almost embedding itself into the wood. Holly carefully un-wrapped the chain, and that allowed her to pull the necklace free. She saw that on the chain was a locket. Intrigued, Holly put the locket into her pocket, and then returned to join her co-workers.

Holly was jolted back to the present for a moment when she hit a dip in the road. She felt for the locket that now hung from her neck. It had become a source of comfort for her. She found herself toying with it, opening and closing the pages. She gently rubbed her fingers over the etching on the cover as she thought back to the way she discovered its beauty.

The evening of the day she had found the locket, she sat at her kitchen table and gave it a closer inspection. The metal looked to be brass, and she could see that there was a design etched into the front, although it was so tarnished that it was difficult to make out any detail. She had nothing to clean the necklace with inside the small trailer that she was staying in. She knew that Brandon and Travis, who were sharing a nearby trailer, wouldn't have anything either, but maybe their landlords, the Nolans, would. She decided to walk down to their house to ask.

Harry and Dottie Nolan were just returning home from a day out shopping in Douglas, a town about sixty miles from there. Harry unfolded himself from the driver's side of the car and grimaced as he stretched his arms over his head. He was a tall man in his mid-sixties with close-cropped salt and pepper hair; his eyes were a clear cornflower blue.

Dottie emerged from the passenger side laughing playfully. She was always amused at how Harry had to contort himself to fit inside their compact car. Dottie didn't have that problem. She was short but curvaceous with short brown hair, which framed a pretty face. Her captivating smile and large brown eyes were warm, welcoming.

As Holly approached the house, Dottie called out to her. Harry lifted the trunk latch and began to lift out the bags of groceries. Holly offered to help and soon they were all gathered in the kitchen shelving the groceries.

"That was quite a load of food for just two people," Holly commented.

"When you live out here in the boonies, you have to be prepared. We usually go into town about twice a month, so we stock up," Dottie replied.

On his way out of the room, Harry commented, "Twice a month is about all I can handle."

Dottie grinned and rolled her eyes at Harry's back. Turning to Holly, she asked, "Want to stay for dinner? It's nothing fancy, just leftovers."

"Sure. I don't have much in the trailer. I haven't had a chance to go shopping yet. Brandon and Travis promised to take me this weekend."

After dinner, Harry retired to the living room to watch his favorite TV show. Dottie rose to clear the table. At that instant, Holly remembered the locket.

"Oh, Dottie, I have a favor to ask. I found this old piece of jewelry down by the creek. I think it's brass, but it could be gold. Do you have something to clean it with?"

"Let me see it. Did you bring it with you?"

"I have it right here in my pocket." Holly pulled the necklace out, handing it to her.

"Wow, this is in pretty bad shape. I think it's an antique, definitely made of brass. I probably have some brass cleaner under the sink. Let me look. "Dottie peered into the cabinet and pulled out a small plastic container of brass and copper cleaner.

"The instructions are on the label. Take this with you because it might take more than one application to get it cleaned up. Try this old toothbrush," Dottie suggested, handing Holly the supplies.

After dinner, back at her trailer, Holly sat at the kitchen table and began to polish the locket. It was shaped like a small book with a hinge on one side and a clasp on the other. The clasp was loose, so as she cleaned it the inside unfolded easily, releasing dirt and debris. There were two inner pages with places for pictures or mementos. The inside covers provided room for two additional photos.

There were remnants of photographs inside the oval frames of the front and back covers. One revealed the lower half of a man dressed in a dark Victorian suit. The other was a very faded image of a little girl holding a doll. The two inner pages were hard to pry apart, but when they opened, Holly saw that each held a lock of hair, one blonde, one black.

The front cover of the locket was beautifully etched with an intricate design featuring a large lily in the center, surrounded by a tangled frame of ivy. As the design became clear, Holly felt that this must have been a cherished piece of jewelry to its original owner.

Once the locket and chain were polished, Holly was delighted with the results. The clasp needed to be bent back into shape in order for the locket to stay shut. She retrieved a pair of needle-nose pliers from the toolbox she kept in her truck, and carefully repaired the clasp.

Holly was not one to wear jewelry regularly, but the locket called to her. She fastened it around her neck. At once, she experienced a sense of warmth and familiarity much like the feeling she had experienced when she walked through the living room of the old stone cottage at the Hideaway Ranch.

A gust of wind lashed against the door of the truck. Holly released the locket, unknowingly leaving the clasp slightly ajar. She put both hands back on the wheel as she approached a fork in the road. She turned left toward Turkey Creek.

This meant having to cross the usually dry wash, which was now flowing with about a foot of water. The rain was still pouring. The road through the twenty-foot span across the creek was well worn from frequent use. She saw no problem in crossing it with such a shallow flow of water. As she started across the truck began to sputter. Then the engine died.

"Shit!" Holly turned the key in the ignition. "Start, damn it!"

She pounded on the steering wheel. She turned and pulled her jacket from the storage area behind the seat and put it on. After popping the hood, she stepped out of the truck, becoming soaked in the downpour. Sloshing her way to the front of the vehicle, she raised the hood and began to inspect the engine.

Steam rose from under the hood, and the rain sizzled as it landed on the hot surface of the engine. Holly poked around looking for obvious problems, such as a broken belt or damaged hose. Nothing seemed amiss.

She knew enough about engines to maintain her truck, to fix minor problems as they occurred. It had only taken one extremely aggravating experience with mechanical failure while camping in the wilderness to learn how important basic knowledge of her truck was. The day after she had returned home, she signed up for a basic auto mechanics class and since then had put the information she'd learned to good use. However, the rain made any chance of diagnosing the problem almost impossible.

After closing the hood, she knelt near the front tire on the driver's side to check the undercarriage. As she bent down, she heard a loud rumbling coming from upstream. Realizing that it was a flash flood that she was hearing, and that it was headed her way, Holly's heart began to pound. Her eyes darted around in search of an escape.

She had no time to think, a torrential wall of water came down toward her and the truck. In an instant, she was swept off her feet, into the raging water. She tried to fight the current, but the water was moving too fast. She looked back to see that her pickup was now several yards behind her, but was moving toward her.

She struggled as she tried not to panic. Her jacket became tangled in a pile of debris, jerking her back into a rocky embankment. As her head hit one of the rocks, her world turned dark.

Chapter Two

Joseph felt the tingle of electricity in the air, the hair on his arms and the back of his neck bristled. He could almost taste the strange odor of ozone on the breeze. The wind was beginning to whirl around him as another clap of thunder rang in his ears.

His hair blew back with such force that he threw his arms up letting out a primal scream as a rush of exhilaration surged through his body. As if on cue, another flash of lightning fractured the darkening sky. Joseph rapidly clicked off a series of shots with the camera that hung from his neck.

The drizzling rain was now forming into solid sheets coming down with ever-increasing force. Tucking his Nikon under his shirt and shielding his eyes from the rain, he rushed over to the tripod where his other camera was mounted. He grabbed his camera bag out from under the tarp, which was settled over the tripod. Slinging the bag over his shoulder, he folded up the legs of the tripod. He left the tarp over the camera, scooped it up, tucked it under his arm, and then jogged toward his SUV.

Opening the back of his Jeep he stowed his equipment with less care than normal, and slammed the hatch shut as he made for the driver's-side door. Once inside, he paused to wipe the rain off his face with his sleeve, and removed the camera from around his neck. He placed it in its fabric case, which he had left on the passenger seat.

Grinning, he thought about that last bolt of lightning. That could be his money shot. As an amateur photographer trying to pursue a career in the business, a goal of his was to have one of his photos chosen to be included in an issue of *Arizona Highways* magazine. They always had such awe-inspiring images of Arizona's lightning storms. His gut told him that at least one of the series of photos he took today would rival any of those.

Maybe Jimmy, the weather forecaster on the local channel, had it right last night when he predicted that today's storm would be a doozy. Joseph was glad that he had taken the day to drive down to the Chiricahuas from Tucson.

The sky lit up, briefly illuminating the encroaching gloom. Joseph automatically began to count "one one-thousand, two one-thousand, three…." The truck shook with the force of the anticipated clap of thunder.

"Damn that was close." Digging out his keys from the front pocket of his jeans, he inserted the key into the ignition. He switched on the wipers, the lights, and the defogger. Reaching over, he stowed the camera case under the passenger seat and pulled the seatbelt across his chest.

The satellite radio was playing Nickleback's *If Today Was Your Last Day*. Joseph sang along "Would you find that one you're dreamin' of? Swear up and down to God above that you'd finally fall in love-If today was your last day." As the song came to an end, he chuckled to himself. *It might be my last day if I don't get off this mountain.*

Starting the engine, he began his descent. The defogger wasn't working well enough to keep the windshield clear, so he rolled down the windows. The breeze on his damp skin gave him a slight chill.

He inhaled deeply catching the sweet scent of the rain soaked high desert. There was nothing like the blend of creosote, juniper, and chaparral, along with an assortment of other aromatic plants. As he pulled onto Turkey Creek Road, he could hear the sound of rushing water off to his right. Turning his head briefly, he looked to see if he could find the source, but the trees and brush blocked his view.

He assumed that Turkey Creek was filling fast. It hadn't been raining that hard for that long here on this side of the mountain, but the storm had rolled in from the north, so it was likely this was a flash flood resulting from earlier rains at a higher elevation. He hoped that he could beat the water to the bridge that crossed the creek.

Joseph was a native Arizonan; he knew about the danger of flash floods. The dry, sandy soil doesn't soak up water quickly, so heavy rains can produce flood conditions very rapidly, without warning. Dry channels, ditches, and lakebeds will fill swiftly. The water can be strong and violent, sometimes creating a wall ten to thirty feet high.

Everyone is warned repeatedly not to stop their vehicles in a creek bed or wash, even if it doesn't look like rain. In town during the monsoon season, there were always people who ventured into flooded washes even after the city had put up signs warning against crossing them. Because so many of these folks ended up stranded, and some even drowned, Arizona had implemented the Stupid Motorist Law, which states that any motorist who becomes stranded after driving around barricades to enter a flooded stretch of roadway may be charged for the cost of their rescue.

Tuning his radio to the local weather channel, Joseph listened to an update. The forecaster was predicting a convergence of storms over Tucson. It seemed he would be traveling with the rain. He might even have to stay the night in one of the motels in Benson.

He sure hoped not. If he did, he would have to call his cousin Sophie. He would ask her to check in on their grandmother. Nonna might need a hand closing the heavy wooden shutters on her windows and securing the patio furniture.

Up ahead on the right, he spotted, out of the corner of his eye, a flash of red. Something, probably a vehicle was moving. As he drove further down the road, he watched a red pick-up come into view. Ordinarily the sight of a truck on one of the many ranch roads would not have held his attention, but this one, while traveling parallel to him, was facing the wrong direction

He realized the truck was likely being pushed by a wall of water. It seemed he had been right about the flash flooding. There was no way to tell from this distance whether there was anyone in the cab of the truck.

Spying a stand of mailboxes on the side of the road Joseph slowed down in hopes that there would be a driveway or road that would take him in the direction of the pickup. There, just before the mailboxes was a street sign. He turned onto the road. *I hope I'm not getting myself into a messy situation. I wonder if I should call nine-one-one.*

Joseph rolled up the passenger side window to keep the rain from pouring in now that he had changed direction. Leaving the driver's-side window down and turning the radio off to hear any cries for help, he leaned out the window as the SUV bounced and jostled down the dirt road.

The sound of the water coursing down Turkey Creek drowned out all other sounds. The beams of his headlights were caught and reflected by the water up ahead. He would have to turn left soon to follow the red truck. However, there was nothing but brush, rocks and scattered pine trees in either direction. No road or even a path was visible.

I'm going to have to stop and have a look around. He brought his truck to a halt, put it in park, and climbed out. Walking to the edge of the wash, he looked downstream.

That truck looks a lot further away than I first thought. Joseph stood there trying to decide what he should do next. Driving along the side of the creek was out of the question, even with his four-wheel drive. He might have chanced it if it hadn't rained so heavily. Ephemeral puddles formed from the rain and its corresponding runoff. They could disguise the land such that what appeared to be a shallow puddle might actually be a hole several feet deep. He had no intention of getting himself stranded out there.

Although the rain was beginning to ease up, becoming more of a drizzle than a downpour, Joseph was still getting soaked. His shirt was clinging to his body, and he was getting cold. The temperature had dropped considerably in the last hour or so.

I wonder what time it is. Glancing down at his watch, he saw that it was almost 4 o'clock. *I should be on the road, not chasing after a drifting truck. This is insane!* He would go back to his SUV, call nine-one-one, and let the sheriff's department deal with the problem.

Turning around, he started back to his vehicle. The rain and wind were now hitting him in the face, so he brought his left forearm up to his forehead to shield his eyes and turned his face into the protection of his arm. The ground was very slippery, and his hiking boots were now heavy with mud. His left bootlace had come untied, so he knelt to tie it.

Looking over toward the wash, he saw a piece of yellow fabric stuck in a mesquite bush. Curious, he moved toward it for a closer look. He tried not to get too close to the waters' edge as he squatted down at the base of the bush. He saw that the scrap of yellow looked to be clothing of some sort. It was very bright, not at all faded by sun or wind. The garment hadn't been in the bush for long.

It hung from a tangle of debris that was wrapped and twisted into the trunk. Part of this object dangled into the water below. Clods of dirt at his feet began to crumble and fall into the running water. The creek looked to have a good six feet of water in it, maybe more. At least it didn't appear to be rising; it would have to gain three or maybe four feet of water before it spilled beyond the boundary of the wash.

Against his better judgment, Joseph lay down on his stomach. Arms outstretched, he leaned down over the embankment to examine the rubble around the base of the mesquite. His hand felt something soft, the unmistakable feel of human flesh. It was an arm.

My God, it's a body. Still holding on to the appendage he shouted. "Hey, down there, can you hear me?" Joseph leaned a bit further over the edge to listen. There was no reply. "I'm going to get you out of there."

Not thinking about his next move, he reached down with both of his hands feeling for the other arm. He had to lift and turn the body to do this, ripping the yellow windbreaker, which was impaled on the mesquite. The jacket partially supported the weight of the person wedged against the slope.

Maneuvering his hands into place under the dangling arms, he lifted upward. The body began to move toward him. He pulled with all his might. The dead weight as well as the limpness of the arms worked against him. As he heaved, the arms would rise, and he would almost lose his grip.

Joseph transferred himself into a kneeling position, holding fast to the victim, his adrenaline pumping. He moved his right hand down the torso of the body, feeling for something to grasp, maybe a belt. There was nothing but smooth fabric. It would have to do. He grabbed as much of the material as he could hold, and with his left forearm under the left arm of the body and his right hand holding the clothing, he lifted upward.

After a couple of attempts, he had pulled what appeared to be an adult female up over the edge, onto the creek-side. She was covered in sludge. She lay there unmoving. The woman was either dead or unconscious.

He would not - could not - panic. He had taken a basic first aid course that included CPR training a few years back. He hoped he could now recall what he had learned. He leaned over the woman placing his fingers on her neck to check for a pulse while he rested his arm on her chest feeling for the rise and fall of

15

breathing. Her breathing was shallow and she had a weak pulse. She was alive, for now. He had to get some help. Joseph didn't want to leave her, but he had to get his phone from the Jeep.

He took off his shirt and wadded it up into a ball intending to place it beneath her for a pillow. As he lifted her head, he spied a necklace lying in the mud under her neck. He moved it aside. Carefully, he laid her head on the makeshift pillow, making sure to tilt her head to the side to prevent choking if she vomited. He took one last look at her before sprinting to his SUV.

Back at the Jeep, he opened the hatch, found his metal camera case, unlatched it and pulled out his cell phone. He grabbed his emergency road-side kit, slammed the hatch shut, and then opened the driver's side door and flipped on his hazard lights. Jogging back to the creek, he dialed nine-one-one. He listened as the phone rang; once, twice, then, "Nine-one-one, what is your emergency?"

"My name is Joseph Romano. I'm on North Whitetail Road about a quarter of a mile off Turkey Creek Road. It's just before the turnoff to Diamondback Guest Ranch. I just pulled a girl out of a flooded creek. She's breathing but unconscious. There could be other people too. I saw a red pickup in the water."

"All right, sir, is this the call-back number that we can reach you at?"

"Yes."

"What is the approximate age of the victim?"

"Late teens to mid-twenties."

"Besides being unconscious, does she have any obvious injuries, any bleeding?"

"Not that I've seen. I didn't get a really good look at her yet. I made sure she was breathing, after that I went back to my truck to get my cell phone."

"Are you able to remain with the victim until the emergency services arrive?"

"I'm heading back that way now. I'll be here; my Jeep is parked by the creek. I turned my hazard lights on."

"The truck you mentioned, is that in the same area?"

"Yes, but it's downstream. I can't get to it."

"Okay, Mr. Romano. Remain calm. Keep your phone on and close to you. Help will be there soon."

He ended the call, pocketed his phone, and bolted back to the girl's side. He dropped to his knees to look her over. Her condition appeared unchanged. It was easy to see that she had no open wounds or obviously broken extremities because she had little clothing on.

She wore a tank top, bike shorts and hiking boots. The torn windbreaker was still hanging from her left arm, but was not in any shape to provide warmth or insulation from the elements. He slid the windbreaker off, checking the pockets for any form of ID. They were empty. There were no other pockets to check. If the red truck were hers, then maybe her purse or wallet was in it.

Joseph unzipped the emergency kit and began pulling out various items. When Nonna asked him that morning if he had his first-aid box with him, he had brushed her off, telling her that he hadn't taken it out of the Jeep since she had given it to him. *Damned if she weren't right again. Oh - oh that reminds me. I definitely have to call Sophie.*

Sorting through the items, he removed the thermal blanket from the plastic packaging. He laid it across her, tucking the edges under carefully so as not to jostle her any more than necessary. Then he took a moment to smooth the blanket's wrinkles before reaching for a rain poncho, and throwing it over his head. The poncho gave Joseph some relief from the rain which continued to fall.

He picked up the flashlight and loaded the AA batteries. Punching the on-button, he checked to make sure it worked. He placed it near her head so he could easily find it. If it took very long for help to get there, he would need that light.

Joseph saw that there was an LED safety strobe included in his kit. He glanced around for a place to set the beacon. A few feet to his right sat a large boulder. It would provide a stable surface up above the mud. After zipping up the pack, Joseph hopped to his feet and walked over to the rock. Flipping the switch, he turned on the strobe then set it down. It emitted red pulsing light as it rotated. *If they don't see that, they're blind.* He went back to the woman.

His shoulder muscles were beginning to ache from the cold and his earlier exertion. He stretched and rotated his shoulders and neck. As he did so, he caught sight of the pickup, still hung-up down the creek. Joseph moved closer to the edge of the wash to get a better look.

There was no sign that anyone had emerged from the truck. Nor could he see any movement indicating that anyone was trying to get out. He decided to walk a little closer toward it. While doing so, he could look up and down the wash for anyone else that might have gotten into trouble.

Joseph walked about eighty feet in the direction of the truck, gazing back at the girl every so often. He went no further, not wanting to get too far away from her. Reversing his steps, he walked upstream, making a quick stop to check her condition before he continued along the creek-side. He saw no sign of other victims. Going no further than he did downstream meant that he was soon back by the girl's side. Now that there was nothing else he could do, he sat down cross-legged, feeling the strain in his thighs as he did so. *My three days a week at the gym didn't prepare me for this.*

Smoothing her hair from her face, he had a chance to take a better look at her features. Her skin was pale under the dirt caked on her cheeks and chin. He pulled the emergency kit closer, opened it, and rummaged for the package of wet-wipes. He tore it open and used one of the cloths to begin cleaning the mud off her face.

As the mud dissolved, a sprinkle of freckles appeared across the bridge of her nose. She was a pretty girl with delicate bone structure and a small turned up nose. She looked angelic just lying there, almost like a young child.

Gradually, the movement of Joseph's hand slowed until he was almost caressing her face. He shoved the dirty wet-wipes in the back pocket of his jeans. Leaning down over her, he pulled the blanket up a little further under her chin. As he re-tucked the blanket around her, he saw the necklace. He picked it up and cupped it in his hand.

Staring at it, he noted that it was a locket shaped like a book. The clasp that held it shut was open so that he could see old photos and locks of hair behind the tiny glass shields that had protected them from the muddy water. He wiped the surfaces of the locket with a corner of the blanket then shut it closed.

"I don't want this to get lost. I'll take care of it for you," he whispered. Joseph put the necklace into his pocket. "Who are you? What happened to you? What are you doing out here?"

As the words passed his lips, a chill moved through him, which had nothing to do with the weather. He turned the words over in his mind. He realized he hadn't seen another car, nor had he heard the sounds of one. If he hadn't seen that glimpse of the red truck and followed it, in an admittedly foolhardy attempt to be of some assistance, she would still be hanging there.

Worse, her jacket could have given way; ergo, she would have ended up in the water. His heart clenched at the thought of her dying out here all alone. *Is someone worried because you aren't home yet?* As the thought came to him, he almost reached for his cell phone to call someone. He felt his face flush with embarrassment even though there was no one around to see how flustered this girl made him.

Anxiety threatened him as he stroked her forehead. She was so silent, so unmoving. He wondered if he were too late, if he had done too little to save her. If it weren't for the slight rise and fall of her chest under the blanket, he would think she was dead. The strands of brown hair which had escaped her ponytail began to entwine themselves around his fingers, but he didn't stop his soothing gesture.

At this point, he wasn't sure if he was soothing her or himself. It seemed silly to be worrying over "what if's" but the image of her drowning in the swiftly flowing water had insinuated its way into his mind, he couldn't let go of it.

Unconsciously he began humming. Eventually, the humming became words. He sang the song in a hushed tone, unsure why it seemed so important to actually utter the words aloud. He didn't know if she could hear them, but once he began singing, his posture relaxed, and his eyes closed. He allowed the song to work its magic on him.

> "There's a form at the casement, the form of her true love, and
> he whispers with face bent, 'I'm waiting for you, love'
> Get up on the stool, through the lattice step lightly,
> and we'll rove in the grove while the moon's shining brightly."

This lullaby was one he remembered from his childhood. No one had sung it to him, and he couldn't recall anyone teaching it to him. His mother told him that he used to sing it to himself when he was upset; it seemed to soothe him. He thought it had been relegated to his childhood memories along with his baseball glove and dreams of playing centerfield for the Yankees.

But from the ease with which the words flowed from him, the song was not as far in the past as he thought. He had never envisioned himself singing it again, let alone that he would sing it to an unconscious stranger he'd just rescued.

"Merrily, cheerily, noiselessly whirring,
swings the wheel, spins the wheel, while the foot's stirring.
Spritely and lightly and merrily ringing,
trills the sweet voice of the young maiden singing."

It seemed strange to be having such protective feelings for this girl. Yet there was a sense of rightness to his attachment that later Joseph might think to question. But now, here in the moment, he simply gave into that feeling, singing the lullaby over and over.

The rain had subsided. The lightning had moved west, toward Tucson. The clouds had parted, and now he could see patches of cerulean sky. Typical of a monsoon storm, the rain had come and gone in a matter of hours. The birds were now chirping, which generally indicated that the storm had passed.

Joseph heard sirens in the distance. He hoped they were coming for the girl. As he listened they became increasingly louder. He stood and looked west down toward the main road. Within minutes, he spotted flashes of red lights approaching on Turkey Creek Road.

Soon the emergency vehicles rounded the corner onto Whitetail Road. The Sheriff's car led the line of vehicles followed by an EMT truck and an ambulance. As they pulled in behind Joseph's Jeep, he began waving his arms above his head, yelling, "Hey, she's over here!" People poured out with the deputy and one of the paramedics coming toward him as the others gathered their equipment.

The paramedic, a fellow in his mid-forties with a head of bushy dark hair and black framed glasses knelt beside the girl and pulled the blanket aside as he began taking her vital signs. Joseph felt compelled to stay by her side, watching the paramedic's every move. The deputy, a tall sturdy man of fifty-something, wearing dark glasses and a cowboy hat stood by with his clipboard tucked under one arm. Failing to get Joseph's attention, the officer tapped him on the shoulder.

"I'm Deputy Howard. Are you the guy that made the nine-one-one call?"

"Yes, I did."

"So your name is Joseph Romero?"

Joseph nodded yes. He was distracted by the flurry of activity surrounding the girl as the other paramedics began preparing her for transport.

"Do you know this young lady?"

"No. I just came across her when I noticed the pickup floating down Turkey Creek."

"Pick up?"

"There's a little red truck in the creek over there," Joseph indicated, pointing downstream. "I saw it as I was driving down off the mountain. When I drove out here, I looked around for the driver. After a few minutes I spotted her. She was dangling over the edge of the wash; her jacket hung up on a tree branch. I pulled her up, and called nine-one-one."

"Has she been unconscious this whole time?"

"Yes."

"Did she have any ID on her? A purse or backpack maybe?"

"I didn't find anything."

The paramedics, there were four of them, two men and two women, were now toting the litter down the slope. The deputy and Joseph backed out of the way. Joseph felt a tugging in his chest as they put distance between him and the girl.

Watching them lift and place her onto the litter brought home to him the fact that they would be taking her away. He might never know her name or see her again. He didn't understand why it mattered so much to him, why his heart was reacting in this painful way.

Deputy Howard led Joseph by the arm directing him to the wash. "Where exactly was she?"

Joseph moved a few feet to his right and squatted down pointing to the mesquite and the broken limb. "There. I would never have seen her if her jacket hadn't been bright yellow."

"Okay, Mr. Romano I'll need you to fill out a form for me. Let's go back to your Jeep."

As they turned around, Joseph didn't see the paramedics carry the girl to the waiting emergency vehicle, but he heard a door slam and an engine turn over. He turned to look just as the ambulance made a U-turn before it drove off. Joseph whipped around as he hurried to catch up with the deputy.

"Where are they taking her?"

"Most likely to the trauma center at University Medical Center in Tucson. UMC is best equipped to handle a head injury."

Deputy Howard pulled a form from the stack of papers attached to his clipboard and placed it on the top. He handed the clipboard to Joseph.

"Here you go. When you're done, just leave this in the front seat of my car."

"Should I pick up my equipment or do you need me to leave it here?"

"What equipment?"

"Basically everything you see is part of my emergency kit."

"Leave it here for now. We'll give you a call. I'll let you know when you can pick it up."

"But I live in Tucson."

Shrugging, the deputy walked away.

Joseph set the clipboard on the hood of his Jeep and proceeded to fill out the form. When he was finished, he walked over to the deputy's car, opened the driver's-side door and set the clipboard and the deputy's pen on the seat.

He looked around for the deputy; not seeing him; he left. *UMC, huh? Sophie works at UMC.*

Deputy Howard stood on the bank of the creek opposite the red truck. The water level was still much too high to navigate it on foot. The fire department would have the right equipment for the job. He would have to wait until they arrived.

From his vantage point looking down into the cab, he saw no bodies or any sign of a car seat. The bed of the truck was empty. Hopefully, he thought, no one else had been in the truck. If there were others, they too must have been swept into the water. He kept his eye out for other possible victims as he continued to walk along the edge of the creek.

The radio on his shoulder crackled. It was Dispatch calling to let him know that the Sunsites Fire Department had arrived. He headed back toward Whitetail Road. "Tell them to head west along the wash, I'll meet them."

Within minutes, he could see them jogging toward him, carrying their paraphernalia. After directing them to the truck and reminding them to look for personal belongings as well as the truck's registration, he resumed his search.

He found nothing, so he decided to go see if the fire department had any better luck.

"So, Howard, we're just finishing up. We didn't find anyone, but we did find this backpack ... and here's the registration. It was in the glove box."

"Thanks Larry." Throwing the backpack over his shoulder, the deputy nodded at the firefighters as he took off for his car. He clicked on his radio to let communications know they should call a tow-truck. As he walked he began to process the afternoon's events

This could have been much worse. Lucky for her that the guy saw her truck and stopped to investigate. I'm glad I can tell the family that she is alive. I hate having to tell people their loved one is dead.

At his car, Deputy Howard opened the door and picked up the clipboard from the seat. He sat down and skimmed the form Joseph had filled out. It appeared to have all the pertinent information. He put it aside and picked up the backpack from the ground where he had set it. Starting with the outside pockets, he searched the bag.

In the mesh pouch was a mostly empty water bottle, in the right front pocket was a cell phone. In the left pocket, he found a couple of pens and a wallet. Opening the wallet, he found a driver's license. The photo, height, and weight all fit the girl. He felt safe in concluding that the backpack belonged to her.

Resuming his search of the wallet, he found a medical card, a debit/credit card, a student ID, and $40 in cash. There were also a few photos, some scraps of paper with grocery lists and other random notes.

He knew the hospital would need her name as well as the details of her insurance. He called Dispatch getting right to the point. "I have an ID for the unconscious girl found out at Whitetail Road. Her name is Holly Montgomery, age twenty-two. I have her medical card; she appears to be a registered student at NAU. I need you to find out where they transported her then relay this information to that hospital."

After passing along the information, he took a quick look at the registration to make sure the truck was registered in the girl's name. He opened the backpack and sorted through it. He pulled out a pair of pants, followed by a long sleeved shirt, a notebook, a sketchpad, a small food storage container, an empty potato chip bag, and an apple with a large bite taken out of it.

Returning all of the items to the backpack, he came across the cell phone again. *If she is like my daughter, she stores everything in her phone. Maybe she has an emergency contact listed.* There was one emergency number listed. He dialed it, but it went immediately to voice mail. After leaving a short message, he put the phone back in the backpack and set it aside.

The deputy reached for his briefcase. He opened it and took out the incident report. He began to fill it out. It had been a long day; he was missing his regular afternoon coffee break. He pulled his thermos from the drink holder, lifted the lid and took a big swig.

After filling out his paperwork, he stepped out of the car, grabbed the backpack and went around to the back of the vehicle. Howard popped the latch opening the trunk. He placed the backpack inside, and removed his crime scene kit. Although this assuredly looked like an accident, he still needed to process the scene. He closed the trunk and headed over to the area where the girl was found.

As Joseph drove through the pelting rain, he felt drained. A jumbled collage of random thoughts and images ran through his mind. The girl's face, the photos he took that day, his emergency kit that Nonna gave him that was now in the hands of the Sheriff, and whether or not he would get it back, the song he sang to the girl….

He looked at the clock on the dashboard "God I'm so late, I've got to call Sophie." He dug his cell phone out of his back pocket and dialed her number. She answered right away.

"Where are you? We were getting worried."

"I've been playing Superman."

Sophie laughed.

"No, really, I just pulled this girl out of a flooded wash."

"Was she cute?"

"Actually, once she's cleaned up I think she will be."

"So, are you serious? Did you really save a girl's life? Is she going to be okay? Oh, my God, are *you* okay?"

"Yes, I'm serious, and I'm fine. I'm not so sure about her, she was unconscious when they took her away."

Sophie started to say something, but it was muffled. He heard her say "He's fine; he's fine. I don't know all the details. Let me ask him."

"Who's there with you?"

"I'm at Nonna's."

"Oh, good, I was calling you to see if you could check up on her because I'm running so late. While you're there will you close the shutters and bring in the patio furniture? Is it storming there yet?"

"Yeah, we are getting hit pretty hard. I took care of everything. I've been here all afternoon. But, I want to know more about your adventure."

"I'll tell you all about it tomorrow. I'm really feeling rattled right now. I think they are taking the girl to UMC. I'll want to follow up on her condition. I gotta let you go. I'm getting ready to turn onto Highway One-ninety-one. It's still raining here. According to the radio forecast I'll be heading into worse weather." Joseph didn't feel much like talking to anyone, he wanted to be alone with his thoughts. He didn't want Sophie to know just how unsettled he felt, so he covered with banter. "Hey, maybe I'll find a few more damsels in distress on the way home."

"Make sure you get their phone numbers."

"I will if they're conscious."

Sophie chuckled.

Joseph's grin faded after his conversation with his cousin ended. He just couldn't get the picture of the girl lying there on the ground out of his mind. Veiling this image, he heard his own voice singing, "And he whispers with face bent, "I'm waiting for you, love."

Chapter Three

Holly was motionless, swaddled in a cocoon of darkness. Slowly, she became more aware of her surroundings. There was a dim flicker of light. She felt warm; the surface beneath her was soft. Where was she? How did she get here?

Her mind raced in circles trying to fix on an answer. She remembered leaving the ranch, and the storm, but nothing else. Maybe she had been in an accident. Tentatively, she wiggled her toes, then her fingers. She shifted restlessly. Although she could move, her body felt strange, weightless. There was no pain. That was a good thing. Wasn't it? She wanted to open her eyes to look around yet she was afraid of what she might see.

As she lay there contemplating, she began to hear soft sounds. First a crackling and snapping redolent of a campfire, then overlaying that, a rustling of fabric and a creaking like that of a rocking chair. Within moments, those sounds were drowned out by the tap, tap of boots walking across a wooden floor.

Holly froze. Footsteps approached. She was frightened though she didn't know why. If she was in a hospital, which she suspected was the case, she would wake to find herself in the care of professionals - and her friends would surely be there to lend their support.

At least Cassie would be there; she could always count on Cassie and Cassie's family. Ever since the accident that had claimed the lives of Holly's parents, Cassie's family had been there for her. Being an only child, Holly had no siblings. Her living grandparents resided in Ireland. They were wonderful, but she saw little of them. They were quite elderly and couldn't be persuaded to use modern forms of communication, so letters along with the occasional phone call had to suffice.

The footsteps stopped. A heady cloud of floral fragrance descended from above. The scent enveloped her, casting her thoughts to another time and place. She saw herself as a small child sitting in her mother's lap. Her head buried in the crook of her mother's neck, she seemed to remember breathing in this same aroma of roses and lilies. Holly felt a soft hand brush across her forehead and a familiar voice whisper "Ivy."

Holly's eyes flew open. As she began to focus, she saw hovering over her a woman wearing a black headpiece with a veil. The woman knelt down beside her. Holly struggled to pull herself up to sit. Her eyes darted around the room.

A few feet away, nestled in the corner adjacent to a stone fireplace, an antique platform rocker continued to sway back and forth. The raspy creak echoed against the wooden floor. The chair's movement attested to the fact that the woman in black had just been sitting there.

Holly's focus came back to rest on the woman when she began to lift the veil from her face. The gloved hand pulled the lace back to expose stunningly beautiful features. The woman could not have been any older than Holly herself.

Her skin was fair and unblemished. She had a delicate turned-up nose, blue-violet eyes, and full lips. Long blonde curls framed her face. She wore a long black old-fashioned dress with a high neck and long sleeves. Holly thought it looked like an elaborate costume meant for a Halloween dress-up ball.

"My dear, how are you feeling?"

"Who are you?" Holly managed to ask.

"Darling child, my name is Emeline. In a previous life of yours, I was your mother, and you were my Ivy."

"Okaaay. So, I'm in the middle of a *Twilight Zone* episode…. No, seriously, where am I?"

"We are between here and there."

With an expression of disgust, Holly pushed the blankets down, pulled her feet up and began to swing them off the edge of the chaise. She needed to get up and stretch. She also needed to put some distance between herself and this apparently crazy woman.

As Holly rose, Emeline stood up. She backed away from Holly, to give her more room. She reached out to lend a hand as Holly stood up, but Holly rose abruptly, and brushed past her.

Prowling around the room, Holly noticed that as she put distance between herself and the woman, the scent of her floral perfume dissipated. The room was about the size of a large bedroom. An enormous stone fireplace lit with a blazing fire encompassed one wall, the rocking chair set off to the side. Centered under a shuttered window was a small dining table with two matching chairs. Adjacent to the window, the wall was empty but for a large ornate oval mirror. Arriving back beside the chaise, she noticed Emeline's perfume again.

It's so strange; this scent seems so familiar, but I'm sure I've never smelled it before. Mom never wore perfume. I rarely wear it, and Cassie only wears woody fragrances. It brings up feelings, flashes of memory that can't be mine.

Turning toward Emeline, Holly set eyes on the fire in the fireplace. It occurred to her that she couldn't smell the fire. She walked over to the fireplace. Even as she stood directly in front of it, she couldn't smell smoke. She held her hands outstretched toward the flames, yet she could feel no heat.

Holly spun around to face Emeline; her hair flew about her flushed face, her eyes were wide, and her chest rose and fell rapidly as she gasped, "What the hell is going on?"

Emeline took a few halting steps toward Holly. "You are safe here with me. Do not be afraid, my dear."

Holly moved away, bumping into the rocking chair. She grabbed hold of it before it could fall as she continued to move backward pressing herself into the corner. She shrunk down to the floor, curling herself into a fetal position.

I must be dreaming, or maybe I have a brain injury. Oh, God - maybe I've gone crazy. What if I were kidnapped? I think this woman is insane. What if she's a homicidal maniac? I have to get out of here!

Emeline glanced over at the dining table where a plate of shortbread cookies and a glass of milk suddenly appeared. She stepped toward the table, picked up a cookie and the glass of milk, and slowly approached Holly. She bent down, offering Holly the treats.

"Ivy, these are your favorite. We always made these together when we returned from going to town. You were so impatient waiting for them to cool." Holly remained curled up, not looking at or responding to the strange woman.

Emeline set the glass on the floor off to the side and placed the cookie on top of it. "Oh, my dear child," she said in a faltering voice. She knelt, stroking Holly's hair, muttering indistinct, soothing words.

Against her will, Holly relaxed. The touch of the fingers playing lightly against her scalp soothed her. Her thoughts drifted. No matter how much she willed her mind to focus, to concentrate on why she shouldn't be feeling comforted, she couldn't bring her thoughts under control.

Pictures, images, bits of what seemed like memories flickered through her mind. They appeared like old home movies projected against the inside of her eyelids. Riding in a buckboard... kneeling on a chair with her elbows on the table, the same table that was just off to the left of her now... chasing a chicken in circles around a cast iron water pump...

"Stop," Holly begged in a broken voice. "Stop talking to me, stop touching me, stop treating me like a child, your child. I am *not* your child." Holly raised her head from off her knees; she stared at the woman in front of her. She moved her head out from under the woman's hand. "Just tell me where I am and why I'm here."

The woman rose and backed away. When she reached the chaise, she pushed the blankets aside, lifted her skirts and sat down upon its tufted linen surface.

Once the woman - whatever her name was - was a safe distance across the room, Holly could breathe easier. She felt an immediate sense of relief. Standing and moving a few feet to the right, she sat down in the rocking chair. She kept a close eye on the woman, who was nervously smoothing her skirts.

Watching the fingers as they stroked the fabric Holly felt a wash of sadness come over her. Her eyes filled with tears. Holly couldn't understand why this particular feeling now overwhelmed her. *Those fingers... the fingers that tunneled through my hair... Momma....* Holly whimpered as her heart clenched. She realized in shock that she was looking at the woman, thinking of her as "Momma."

Emeline sat on the chaise fidgeting. Suddenly she stood, looked Holly in the eye and made a proclamation.

"I have searched my head and my heart for an easy way to say this." She stopped, took a deep breath and continued. "I believe - no, rather I *know* - that we are somehow trapped inside my mourning locket."

Chapter Four

Joseph woke to his cell phone ringing. He reached over to pick it up from the bedside table. "Hello?"

"Morning Tesoro, are you home?" Nonna always called him Tesoro, Italian for treasure.

"Yeah, Nonna, I came home late last night."

"Do you want to come over for breakfast? I made your favorite biscotti. The cocoa ones dipped in chocolate."

"Don't tempt me. I have to meet the guys at the gym this morning. What time is it?"

"It's almost eight-thirty."

"Oh God, I have to go, sorry, Nonna."

"Joseph, watch your tongue. Come by when you're through. We will have lunch."

"Okay. I'll see you later."

Joseph set the phone down and pulled on his gym shorts. He headed into the bathroom in order to have a look in the mirror. His hair was standing out all over his head. *That's what I get for going to bed with wet hair.*

He dampened his hair and combed through it, brushed his teeth, then packed a few items in his gym bag. He walked through the house as he pulled a T-shirt over his head. He gathered his wallet and phone and tossed them into the bag. Lastly, he grabbed his keys, as well as his favorite pair of sunglasses before he headed out the door.

His Jeep sat under the carport, covered in mud. "Crap, I have to get to the car wash today." Staring at the Jeep brought the events of yesterday back to mind. Thinking of the girl he became anxious, concerned for her welfare. Later today he'd call Sophie. She'd be asleep now since she worked the night shift at the hospital, but she might have learned something about the girl's condition.

He pulled out of the driveway. Traffic was light. As he drove through the neighborhood, Joseph noted a significant amount of damage from the storm. The power company had trucks out in full force repairing downed power lines. Yards were littered with branches, trash, and roof shingles. People were just beginning to clean up the debris. Some streets were still blocked off with **DO NOT ENTER WHEN FLOODED** signs. He had to take a detour from his usual route to get to the gym. He pulled into the parking lot running about five minutes late.

Joseph walked through the lobby straight to the men's locker room. He put his bag away after grabbing his MP3 player and armband. Jogging down the hallway, he joined his friends on the machines. He jumped on a tread-mill to a barrage of greetings. Before he started the machine, he selected his workout playlist.

When the machine started his thoughts turned to the photos he took yesterday. When he made it home, he would get into his darkroom and start developing the film from his single-lens-reflex camera. While he was waiting, he'd load the images from his digital camera onto his computer.

He couldn't wait to start the editing process, to get a look at the prints. He had a gut feeling about these pictures; he knew he had captured something magical yesterday.

It sure had been a crazy day, racing the storm down the mountain, finding the girl. What was with the almost paternal feelings that overtook him when he sat at her side? She was about the same age as he was, and she was surely pretty enough. He shivered at the idea that he might be experiencing some kind of weird nesting instinct. *Okay, you need to think about something else.*

Next week was going to be a busy one. He had several portrait commissions, and one wedding, as well as two birthday parties. Weddings could be difficult as emotions tended to run high, so he really wasn't looking forward to that gig. Unfortunately, those were the jobs that paid his bills.

He began singing along with the song that was playing on his MP3 player. "You spin me right round, baby. Right round like a record, baby." Joseph lost his stride as he realized just what he was singing. "What the ...." Regaining his footing, he forwarded to the next song. *How the fuck did that song get in my playlist? I don't even like that song. Hell, I don't even own that song. Dead or Alive sucks. Now that stupid tune is going to be stuck in my head all day.*

Running along to the beat of the next song Joseph continued to think about the upcoming week. Soon the earworm took hold again, and he found himself singing "spin me right round" again. The lyrics led to thoughts of the lullaby he sang yesterday to that girl: spinning wheels spinning round. Ugh, he hadn't thought of that song in ages. Now here it was in his head two days in a row.

Wiping his brow with his forearm, he looked up to see a pretty brunette wearing her hair in a ponytail, and dressed in exercise shorts and a tank top. She started jogging on another treadmill. His heart stopped as he briefly thought it was her—the girl he'd rescued. Rationally, he knew it couldn't be her; also, as he stared at the brunette he saw obvious differences between them. He couldn't seem to shake all these reminders of the girl. He wished he at least knew her name. Thinking of her as 'the girl' was annoying.

His circuit ended. He was relieved to leave the brunette behind as he joined his friends Andy, Ryan, and Nick in the weight room. They were slightly ahead of him in their lifting routine, as he had arrived late at the gym. The guys nodded to each other as Joseph settled down to his first machine. Fortunately, he wasn't bothered by any more thoughts of the girl as he focused on his reps and form.

Good-natured bantering flowed between the friends as they retreated to the locker room bound for the showers. While getting dressed Joseph began to tell them about his trip to the mountains and how it ended with the rescue of a girl. His story continued until they were settled into a booth at the juice bar inside the gym. They always stopped for a drink after working out. It allowed them to catch up.

"Where's your cape?" Andy asked.

"Yeah, I didn't see the bat signal over the city last night." Nick ribbed Joseph.

Ryan looked confused. "When did you become the hero? In college, it was always the girls having to rescue you. They helped you write papers on time, do your laundry before you were sockless, and so on."

The guys all jeered at Joseph as he tried to defend himself. "You're doing that again, it looks like you're training to be a sign language interpreter." Ryan mimicked Joseph's hand gestures. It was a mannerism he had picked up from Nonna. Joseph had asked his friends to call him on it if they noticed him talking with his hands. He was trying to stop the annoying habit. He usually found himself gesturing only when he was really excited or really angry. Feeling self-conscious, Joseph shoved his hands into his front pockets.

"Hey guys, I'm telling the truth. There really was a girl, and I really did pull her from a flooded wash."

"Okay, so saying we believe you, was she a babe? Did you get her number?"

"I just told you she was unconscious the whole time! I couldn't tell you what she looked like, because she was covered in mud."

Joseph only felt a small twinge of guilt for lying to his friends. He just couldn't bring himself to share anything more about the girl. He was feeling protective again, and he didn't understand it. He tried to change the subject.

"How hard did you guys get hit by the storm? It looked as if it did some major damage."

"Nope, we aren't letting you off that easily," Nick said. "We want more details. This is the most exciting thing to happen to any of us since Andy proved that what happens in Vegas needs to stay in Vegas."

Laughing at the face Andy made while being reminded of his folly, Joseph insisted that he had told them everything. The topic finally turned to the upcoming football season, and consequently, Joseph's adventure took second place to the question of which team had a better quarterback.

Before he returned home, Joseph stopped at the closest car wash. As he drove the Jeep through it, he checked his phone for new messages. There were no new messages or missed calls. Joseph sighed heavily. He called Nonna to let her know he'd be home within a half-hour.

After arriving home, Joseph emptied the gym bag and gathered up his dirty clothes. His washer and dryer were located just off the kitchen on a small service porch. Emptying the pockets as he sorted the clothes, he found the necklace. He slipped it into his front jeans pocket. *I need to take this to the hospital.* He started a load of laundry, and then proceeded to unpack his cameras. His fingers itched to begin processing everything, but he forced himself to wait.

He walked next door to Nonna's. Their family owned a section of row houses. It had become Joseph's job to manage the family's properties in exchange for living rent-free. Nonna's house shared a wall with Joseph's. Each had its own carport and a small courtyard. The front of the building was shaded by Palo Verde and Mesquite trees.

Joseph hollered out to Nonna as he opened the front door. He was greeted with the delicious smell of herbs and garlic. He took a deep breath. Nonna's house always smelled wonderful. He realized he was starving; he followed his nose to the kitchen.

Nonna was there stirring something on the stove. He walked over to where she stood bending to kiss the top of her head. She turned and smiled at Joseph as she reached up to pat his cheek.

"Tesoro. Sit, sit, you must be hungry. This is almost done. You can begin with the green salad while I finish."

Joseph reached out and snagged a piece of biscotti from a plate on the counter on his way to the table. Around a mouthful of cookie, he mumbled, "I'd rather wait for you." He pulled out a bright red ladder back chair sitting down at Nonna's dining table.

Today she had covered it with a rainbow-colored Mexican blanket, the colors of which were tame compared to the colors and patterns on the chairs and dishware. Nonna was an artist; she loved to surround herself with bright colors and interesting textures.

She joined him at the table, choosing a bright yellow chair in which to sit. She handed him a bowl of warm pasta salad, one of her specialties. As they served themselves and began eating, Joseph told her all about the flash flood and saving the girl.

As he concluded his tale and they finished their lunch, Joseph said, "I'm so confused. I can't seem to get her out of my head. I thought I saw her at the gym this morning. I feel as if I should be at the hospital with her. It physically hurt to be separated from her when they took her away in the ambulance."

Taking a deep breath, he pushed his chair back and stood up from the table. He picked up the dishes and carried them to the sink. "Remember the song that I used to sing when I was little? I thought I had forgotten it, but yesterday when I was sitting with her, waiting for help, it came back to me, and I felt the need to sing it to her. It's all just so weird."

Nonna stood up from the table and approached Joseph, laying her hand on his arm. "That was a traumatic ordeal, anyone would be rattled. You probably just needed to comfort yourself, so you reverted to your childhood. That song was like your security blanket. We never did figure out where you learned it. We were just glad it worked." With a laugh, she turned away as she loaded the dishwasher.

Joseph pulled out the locket and examined it. It wouldn't open because it was encrusted with mud. Nonna walked over to see what he was doing.

"What do you have there?"

"I think this belongs to the girl. I found it in the mud under her neck. I'm going to take it to the hospital later. I think they took her to UMC. I'll talk to Sophie before she goes to work, see if she knows anything."

Nonna reached out, and Joseph placed the locket in her hand. She looked it over, noting that it was in desperate need of cleaning. "You can't return this to her in this condition. Let me clean it for her."

"Sure, thanks. I'm going to go home to work on yesterday's photos. I'll come by and pick it up before I go to the hospital."

Joseph thanked Nonna for lunch, accepted the leftovers that she insisted he take with him, and went home. In his darkroom, he became engrossed in his work. Reaching the 'wash' stage, he set the timer on his watch for twenty-five minutes, and sat down to wait. Drowsiness quickly set in, and he drifted off.

Chapter Five

That settles it. I must be dreaming. Ever since Emeline's pronouncement that the two of them were trapped inside a piece of jewelry, Holly had decided that what she was now experiencing *had* to be a nightmare.

She squeezed her eyes shut and started to count to one hundred, hoping that when she opened them, she would be somewhere other than the strange room. By the time she reached fifty-seven, she lost her patience and abruptly opened her eyes. The woman was still sitting there across from her, staring.

Scowling Holly turned her head away. She took a deep breath and pinched herself hard on the arm. She hardly felt a thing. *Damn, that didn't work either.*

Rubbing her arm where she had pinched herself, she started to question why that hadn't hurt as she expected it to. *I can feel my fingers touching my arm, so why couldn't I feel the pinch?* Slapping her arm, she braced herself for the sting. It didn't come.

So, I can't feel pain. She began to touch her hair, her face, the chair, next she reached out to the logs piled on the hearth. *I can feel the texture. Something must be dulling the pain. I haven't felt any aches or pains from the accident that I'm assuming I had... Hmmm. I must be on some heavy-duty pain killers.*

Laughing at herself, Holly relaxed a bit, leaning back against the chair. She looked around the room with new eyes. *That explains why I can't wake up. But why did my brain conjure up this weird room, and why this woman? If I were going to be alone with someone, why couldn't it be Ian Somerhalder?*

She recalled a book that Cassie had lent to her on the subject of lucid dreaming, the state of being aware that you are dreaming and having some control of events within the dream. Was this happening to her now?

Holly rose from the chair; she began to walk around the room, giving everything a closer inspection. Maybe if she ignored, Emma- what's-her-face, she would just disappear. After all, this was *her* dream, *her* imagination, so she should be able to control it, right?

So maybe I can't control it, but I should be able to have faith that I'm safe. Standing near the table, she saw the cookies. They looked tempting now, so she helped herself to one. She took a bite. It was soft and chewy, but had no taste. She forced herself to swallow as she examined the rest of the cookie. She brought it up to her nose and sniffed.

No smell. It felt and looked like a cookie, why, she wondered, didn't it taste or smell like one? Why would she imagine a cookie that had no taste? If she were going to imagine a cookie, it would be the best tasting cookie ever made.

Turning to her right, she saw a bed in the corner across from the rocking chair. That piece of furniture hadn't been there when she first looked around the room. *My mind must be adding items to the decor. I wonder if this means that unconsciously I know that I will be in here for a while.*

She walked toward the bed. It was an old black iron four-poster bed frame with a sagging mattress layered in quilts. Moving closer her focus narrowed to the top quilt covering the bed. She was drawn to it like a magnet.

The background fabric was buff colored with appliqués in a geometrical, quasi-floral pattern of moss green, ginger, and brick red. She thought it was hideously ugly, not colors she would have chosen yet she couldn't imagine the quilt being any other color. Somehow it just seemed right.

Reaching out to touch the quilt Holly heard a small voice say "mine." She immediately pulled back as she looked around for the source of the sound. There was no one else in the room except for the woman in black who still sat on the lounge observing her.

Taking a step forward, Holly tentatively stretched out her hand. "Mine." This time she realized that the small voice was coming from her own mouth. Gasping Holly clasped her hand over her mouth, stepping back. The bed was suddenly gone.

What the hell is going on here? Cookies that have no taste, beds that appear, then disappear, and suddenly I'm a ventriloquist throwing a creepy little girl voice. I'm freaking myself out now! Maybe it's not just medication. Maybe there is something wrong with my brain. Am I still me? How could I know? Ah, I'll look in the mirror....

She darted for the mirror that hung on the wall and gazed at her reflection. She looked like herself, and none of her inner turmoil shown on her face. A bout of dizziness overcame her. Leaning against the mirror, she rested her forehead on its cool surface, her hands braced on either side of her face. She closed her eyes and took a few deep breaths.

As the spell of vertigo passed, Holly slowly opened her eyes. She turned her head and began to pull back from the mirror. All at once she observed a flash of light and movement at the edge of the frame.

She examined the mirror closely. It was indeed a mirror, though she now saw that it was hinged on one side. On the other side, a latch lay partially hidden by the ornate frame. *Maybe it's a window.* Excited by the possibility that there was activity outside the four walls of her seemingly self-induced prison, she turned to face Emeline.

"I think this mirror is really a window, I saw what looked like a sliver of daylight; and something moved right at the rim of the frame. It looks as if it opens. Did you know that?"

Emeline had been silent as Holly explored. She was reluctant to say anything else since she had declared that she believed they were trapped in the locket that Jonathan had given her. Holly hadn't let her finish her explanation. She had reacted with disbelief, brushing her off as a dream or a hallucination. Now Emeline had her chance to speak.

"Yes, it serves as a window. It is the front of the locket. It opened before, but we cannot open it from this side. They have to open it from the other side."

"Who are they?" "Who is on the other side?"

"The living."

"The living? Does that mean that we are dead?" Icy fingers ran up Holly's spine.

"Merely between worlds."

"I don't understand."

"You will."

Emeline didn't mean to sound ominous, though she realized that her vague answers sounded that way. It was just so hard to explain their bizarre situation. She didn't understand much of it herself. One thing she did know was that all she had to do was remember something with great intensity, and then as if by magic, it would appear. Trappings came and went over and over again.

She also knew that her ability to manifest provisions did not apply to people. She had earnestly remembered every detail of her life with Jonathan and Ivy, yet neither had miraculously joined her, at least not until now. Holly's appearance was not Emeline's doing, not entirely her doing.

Holly came to her willingly when she found herself in mortal danger during the flash flood. Emeline had seen the accident unfold through the mirror window, which was actually the front of the locket. She had called out to Holly-who-was-Ivy, but never expected her sudden appearance on the chaise.

Now Holly regarded her with suspicion, and Emeline would have to be prudent. She needed to find a delicate way to tell her all that she knew.

Holly looked back toward the mirror. That *had* to be her ticket out of there. On the wall, about a foot to the left of the mirror, stood a small dresser that hadn't been there before. Spilling out from the partially open drawers were items of clothing.

Holly approached the dresser and reached for a tiny sleeve. Pulling items from the drawers, she realized that everything in the dresser ostensibly belonged to a small girl. Oddly, Holly felt as though she had seen this clothing before.

She looked over her shoulder, keeping tabs on Emeline. The woman quietly observed as Holly explored. Holly turned her attention back to the dresser, she found that it was no longer there. The space was empty. *Why am I not surprised?*

Now, as Holly surveyed the room looking for other changes, she saw that there was a door that hadn't been there before. Excited, she walked across the room to the door, on the wall where the chaise still sat. The floor creaked as she strode across it.

She observed that the door was made of wooden panels. Something that looked like tar was smeared over the lumber to seal the cracks. Right about eye level was a small rectangular sliding peephole about five inches high and approximately seven or eight inches wide. A knob allowed one to slide the peephole open. Holly wasted no time. She slid the small window open and took a look.

The view before her was one she had seen many times over the summer. She knew immediately where she was. She spun around to take in the room with new eyes. She had to confirm her discovery. She thought back to the first day she set foot in the old abandoned ranch house. The side door faced east. The fireplace was on the south wall. The front door had been on the north.

Something was wrong. Her view from the door a moment ago had been the side yard looking toward a stand of pine trees and the small hill beyond. Everything was right except for the front door. There was only one door now. The other door was missing.

Emeline saw from the puzzled look on Holly's face that something had her baffled. Tentatively, she spoke up.

"What did you see? You seem to be searching for something. May I help?"

"I don't know. If I'm right, we aren't trapped in any old locket; we are in the Hideaway Ranch house. This must have been how it looked when it was first built. This is one crazy dream. Now I'm back in time. That must be why I'm imagining you in that old-fashioned outfit. What I don't get is that there should be a front door over there." Holly pointed at the north wall.

"Indeed, there should be."

As soon as Emeline uttered the words, a door appeared on the north wall. Holly gasped. *How could she be manipulating my dream?* Something else was going on. *Maybe this woman knows more about what is happening to me than I've given her credit for.* "Okay, please tell me everything you know."

Emeline smiled. Finally, Holly was ready to listen.

"Of course, my child. I will tell you, though I must begin at the beginning. Will you hear me out before you ask questions?"

Holly sighed. "Sure. I'm not going anywhere. Tell me your story."

Emeline began.

Chapter Six

"This is how I remember it. In the weeks leading up to the evening I met Jonathan my life was rapidly changing." Emeline walked about the room in a dreamlike state as she talked.

Holly sat down on the lounge and drew her feet up under her to sit Indian style.

Emeline went on, "One morning when summer was at its end and there was an autumn chill in the air, Mother and I walked along Vine Street toward the dressmaker's shop. I detected the sweet smell of apple wood burning in someone's fireplace. I was beside myself with anticipation because we were going to the shop to choose the fabric and patterns for our new gowns. It was my first year attending the ball, the Banker's Ball, and I was overjoyed."

"What exactly is a Banker's Ball?"

"My father launched the Ball in 1879, and that meant that the event was celebrating its fifth year. It was the town's most talked-about social occasion. The dance was really my mother's scheme.

"When she brought the notion forth my father thought it was an epic idea. He invited his most prestigious investors and account holders, along with their ladies, of course. It was profitable for both the bank and his reputation as an astute manager.

"You see; my father was the president of the Old State National Bank. He had been with the bank for more than twenty-five years. He was instrumental in the restoration of the building, which had an impressive new facade reminiscent of a Greek temple with Ionian columns along the front. But, it was his keen mind for business as well as his charismatic personality that made him a success."

Holly rolled her eyes. "I'm sorry I asked. It sounds boring, but I guess if it was the social event of the season…"

"It was indeed." Emeline frowned. "As we entered the dressmaker's shop that morning, it was buzzing with activity. Some women bought their dresses out of town or had them made by other dressmakers, but Mrs. Showrey was a top-notch seamstress, and Mother never went anywhere else for her clothing."

Emeline smoothed her skirt and continued to mill around the room as she talked. Thinking about the beautiful clothes she once owned saddened her. She had been wearing the same black mourning garb for ages it seemed. She sighed, and then continued.

"A girl who worked for Mrs. Showery escorted us to a back room where she had set up a tea cart for us. We settled on the lovely chairs with the rose pattern embroidery. We sipped our tea while we waited for Mrs. Showery to finish with the clients ahead of us."

"This is leading where?"

"I am explaining how we came to be here. I cannot skip the introduction and arrive at the conclusion. Be patient.

"As I was saying, we were surrounded by bolts of divine fabrics. Mother and I discussed possibilities, finally choosing our favorites. Then Mrs. Showery came into the room with a flourish. Her cheeks were flushed from her frenzy to fulfill all of the orders coming in from ball attendees. She always had to hire extra help at that time of year, yet she would never complain. The Ball kept her household afloat for months afterward."

Holly unfolded herself and lay down on the chaise. She put her hands under her head and closed her eyes.

"Are you listening to me?" Emeline stood over Holly with her hands on her hips and a stern look on her face.

"I'm listening. Just thought I had better make myself comfortable. Has anyone ever told you that you are long winded? Could you just cut to the chase?"

"I will have you know that I excelled in oration as a student. This is my story and I will tell it as I see fit. Please listen and do not be rude."

"I apologize. Just get on with it." Holly turned over onto her side and propped herself up on her elbow to watch Emeline, as she again paced as she spoke.

"Mrs. Showrey brought out a book with pictures of dresses. All of the gowns were beautiful. After we poured over the book of patterns in addition to the fabrics, Mother chose velvet the color of garnet with a silk underskirt and a bustle. It would be trimmed with pleats, flounces, ruching, and frills. She also ordered a new corset in the fashionable longer style.

"I was torn between two lovely fabrics. One was the gold brocade with pink flowers, the other, a silk brocade in a cornflower blue. Mother thought the blue brought out my eyes, so I chose the blue. We were each to have a velvet evening hat and kid gloves. We left the shop giddy with expectation."

Emeline glanced over at Holly to see if she was attentive. Holly was still lounging but she had her eyes on Emeline. Satisfied, Emeline resumed.

"At home, Marianne, our cook had prepared a lovely luncheon. There was egg consommé followed by chicken pie with stewed apples with nuts. After our meal, Mama and I retreated to our rooms for a rest. I was in high spirits. I couldn't sleep. After trying to read, I found my mind wandering back to the Ball. When I heard Mama leave her rooms, I rushed to join her."

Emeline paused. She had grown pensive, her thoughts turning to people she would never see again, her parents, grandmother and all the others that she had loved and now missed deeply.

Holly responded to Emeline's change in mood by giving her a nod and a smile. Emeline was grateful for the quiet encouragement. After a couple of minutes, Emeline returned to her tale.

"I asked Mama's permission to invite my best friend Helen and my cousin Darcy over for tea. I could not wait to share our visit to Mrs. Showery's with them. Mother was acquiescent to my request as long as I informed Marianne that we would have extras at teatime. I assured her that I would speak with the cook."

"I like the idea of 'tea time.' Did you have it every day? If your family had a cook you must have been pretty well off."

"Yes, we always had teatime. It was customary. As I explained, my father was an astute businessman. As I was saying, after gaining permission to have guests, I went back to my room to tidy my hair then hurried downstairs.

"I poked my head into the kitchen and called to Marianne. I told her of my plans and requested my favorite almond teacakes as well as her unique herbal tisane. I nodded goodbye then walked along the hallway to the foyer. I lifted my hat, shawl and gloves from their niche on a small pedestal which sat against the wall near the front door. Then I set out for Helen's house."

Emeline sat down at the table. Before her a teacup and saucer materialized out of thin air. Emeline picked up the cup and brought it to her lips.

Holly gasped. "That's some magic trick. If it's safe to drink, I'll have a cup too."

Emeline set the cup down on the saucer. "This has become commonplace to me. I should have offered you a cup. I'm not used to having company." She stared at the small table next to the chaise where Holly lay. Within seconds a cup and saucer appeared there.

Holly watched,, eyes wide. She pulled herself up to sit and peered into the cup. It looked like tea. She reached over and picked it up. Steam rose from the vessel and a sweet almond-like aroma filled her nostrils. She blew on the liquid, and then took a sip. It tasted smooth and flavorful. She smiled. *She's getting better at this.*

Emeline smiled back. Refreshed, she began again. "Helen lived two doors down from our home, which was quite convenient. Helen's mother was out for the day, so she was obliged to ask her governess for permission. After a few moments of negotiation, Helen was granted leave for the afternoon.

"Together we walked around the block to my aunt and uncle's house. Cousin Darcy was a year older than Helen and me. It would be her second time attending the Ball. Even so, she was still very enthusiastic, delighted that Helen and I would be there as well.

"Aunt Vivienne had been rushing about all morning preparing for the Ball, so she was resting. Darcy tiptoed into her mother's room. She soon returned to the parlor where Helen and I waited. She had her cloak and hat in hand. We departed for our house linking arms when we reached the street. We were great friends."

Emeline finished her tea and rose from the table. "Once back in the warm, cozy parlor we sat down to tea. Marianne served the scrumptious treats she had promised. Our conversation centered on the Ball of course. Darcy told us once again of her first year attending the event. It sounded wonderful, everything from the lighted Great Hall to the food and especially the dancing with some of the handsome young men in attendance.

"After we had exhausted the topic of the Ball, at least temporarily, Darcy told us of her recent trip to New York. She had visited other cousins there and she was anxious to share news of the latest trends in fashion and style."

"Are you getting off track? You were going to tell me about meeting this Jonathan. You keep referring to how that led to our circumstances here and now."

"I need to tell you everything. You will not understand how I came to be here if you do not hear the whole story. So, where was I? Oh, I know. One of the cousins had shown Darcy her charm string, a custom which was evidently all the rage among proper young ladies. As soon as a girl was old enough to consider suitors, she could begin a chain of buttons attached to a cord or ribbon.

"Darcy told us that usually one's mother or other close female relative would gift the first button to the girl. This button was called a "touch" button. It was usually a very special button, either by virtue of monetary value or sentimental worth. The young lady would begin adding her own buttons to the string. Once the staggering number of a thousand buttons was achieved, the girl's very own Prince Charming would come to sweep her off her feet.

"Such a romantic notion made the three of us swoon with delight. Unquestionably, each of us would start a string forthwith. Darcy had already planted the seed with her own mother and Aunt Vivienne was searching for just the right button to start off Darcy's charm string."

"Really, a button chain was supposed to produce a Prince Charming? That's such a crock. It's alarming that girls were doing that back then. Of course, even nowadays that whole 'handsome Prince riding in to save the day' thing is still alive and well. Ugh!"

"Must you interject some sort of disapproval at every turn?" Emeline shook her head, turning away from Holly before speaking further. *I love that my girl is here with me, I have been so lonely and I truly missed my little one. This young woman that she is now is so unlike the child I knew. I do not understand her ways, nor do I understand her speech. The time she lives in is so unlike the time I lived in. She is angry and upset, I know that. I would feel the same if I found myself in a strange place with a strange person. I must have patience.* She began again.

"The morning of the Ball I stood in my room admiring the shine of my newly polished boots. Mother knocked on the open door to announce her arrival. In her hand was a large brass perfume button.

"I recognized it. The button was one from Grandmother's old Sunday coat. Mother said that when she was visiting with her mother, she had mentioned my desire to begin a charm string. Grandmother had instantly pronounced that she had just the button to serve as my 'touch' button.

"She produced the beautiful brass button with a rosebud set in a green velvet background. The detail was very fine with high relief. Mother handed me the button and a spool of lovely silk ribbon. I threaded the button onto the ribbon and tied a firm knot. My search for Prince Charming had begun."

Emeline turned to Holly silently daring her to speak out. Holly snickered, but didn't utter a word.

"Father left hours before the Ball to make sure that everything ran smoothly. Mother and I set out in our carriage, stopping next door to collect Grandmother. I was so nervous that when we arrived at the hall I almost fainted from trepidation.

"Grandmother reached for her smelling salts which were in a small vial that hung from her chatelaine. I am averse to the scent of those spirits, so I declined. As we entered the hall, a young man announced our arrival. All eyes were on us as we descended the stone steps into the enormous room.

"Gas lamps as well as candles lit up the gallery, which was divided into three sections. To the left were rows of long tables piled with scrumptious looking comestibles. The dance floor lay before us in the center of the hall, with a raised platform at the far end where a six-piece ensemble was playing a lighthearted tune I recognized as *Sweet Violets*.

"I was bemused by the song choice, as I knew the lyrics to be quite humorous. Although the band played an instrumental version, I could not keep from singing the words in my head." Emeline still remembered the tune, and hummed a few bars.

"To the right of the dance arena, tables were set with seating for ten or twelve guests at each. At the foot of the stairs where we stood was an alcove where a couple of menservants took our coats. A wide lobby gave guests ample room to move from one place to another without disturbing either diners or dancers. Mother, Grandmother and I proceeded to the buffet tables."

Holly yawned. "The whole thing sounds like a blast."

"It was at that moment that I first laid eyes on Jonathan. He was standing at one end of the buffet area, speaking with an older gentleman whom I later learned was his father. Jonathan was deeply engaged in his conversation. I could see by the gesturing of his hands and the consternation in his face that he meant to get his point across.

"He was the most striking man I had ever seen, with jet-black wavy hair that framed a chiseled handsome face. His broad brow, high cheekbones, and full, sensuous lips drew me to stare. Lean and tall, he was quite a figure in his cutaway coat with matching vest.

"I stood mesmerized, unable to hear or respond to Darcy and Helen as they tried to get my attention. When they realized where my gaze had fallen they broke out in girlish, unseemly laughter."

Holly laughed out loud. "Sensuous lips huh? So Jonathan was a hottie." She winked at Emeline. "Go on. Are we getting to the good part?" Emeline was undeterred.

"My friend's chortling seized Jonathan's attention and he looked our direction. I know that I blushed and turned away, but not before I saw his dazzling grin. I was beside myself with embarrassment.

"I corralled the girls, leading them back to our table. My heart fluttered in my chest, and my insides felt as though I had swallowed lumps of clay. We sat struggling to compose ourselves. Our parents, who were making merry with their acquaintances, barely noticed our return.

"Soon after we gained our composure, people began to move on to the dance floor. My mother bade us follow her to the seating area where the ladies sat to fill out their dance cards. A young man walked around the hall, he handed the cards to all of the women. Darcy, Helen and I each took a card.

"The folded card featured a cover which depicted a sketch of the bank as well as the date of the Ball. Inside the card, the music and dance style, whether quadrille, waltz, or reel was listed, with a place to pencil in the name of a partner. This being my first formal dance; my mother had explained to me that young men would ask me for a dance, and then I was to fill out the card accordingly."

"Could you refuse to dance with a guy if you didn't want to dance with him?"

"To simply refuse would have been rude. The polite thing to do would be to explain that one's card was full."

"Hmm." Holly motioned for Emeline to continue.

"We girls sat nervously awaiting the gentlemen, who now sat on the other side of the gleaming Hall. The room fell silent as my father took the stage. The small ensemble had been replaced by a larger chamber orchestra. As Father announced them, the welcome music began. This was the cue for men to drift toward our side of the room.

"Father came to escort my mother to the dance floor. He requested that I pencil him in for a dance. Before my parents could move onto the floor, Jonathan and his father came strolling up to them. My father shook the older man's hand introducing him as Nathanial Evans, a name we all knew well.

"Mr. Evans was one of *the* Evans family for which the city was named. Having left Indiana as a young man, he was now a shipping tycoon with homes in New York, Evansville, London, and Paris. He kept a large account at Old State National.

"He presented his youngest son, Jonathan, telling Father that he had big plans for the boy. I stood behind Mother trying not to look at the son as his father prattled on about his business ventures."

"You're a fine one to talk about prattling on." Holly sighed heavily.

Emeline ignored the comment and sat down in the rocking chair. "Jonathan left his father's side unnoticed, moving around to approach me from behind. Since I was busy trying to ignore him, I did not know that he was standing there until he tapped me on the shoulder.

"I turned around to find him beaming down on me. I felt like butter melting under his gaze. He asked for the next dance, and I could not refuse. When the music began, he led me to the dance floor. It was a waltz, the *Tale of the Vienna Woods*. I will never forget the music or the way I felt as I glided in Jonathan's arms for the first time."

Emeline sat rocking and gazing off in a daze with a dreamy look on her face. Holly squirmed and repositioned herself on the settee.

Finally, Emeline resumed "I was dumbstruck; I hardly knew what to say. Thankfully, Jonathan was an experienced conversationalist. As he spoke I began to relax. He told me of his dream to move west to the Territories, to operate his own ranch. This seemed remarkable for the son of a prestigious businessman, so I inquired as to his father's thoughts on the matter.

"Jonathan's face fell, his mood turned grim as he related the exchange between them when Jonathan had first broached his idea. Nathaniel Evans was not impressed. He had other plans for his youngest son. A vice presidency with a new branch of the shipping company awaited him in the coming years. As far as Nathaniel was concerned, the argument was settled. It was obvious from Jonathan's passion that the issue was far from resolved.

"My dance card was empty save for my father's requested dance, but … after that first dance, Jonathan asked for my card. He proceeded to write his name next to every other available dance. We talked about everything from hopes and dreams to food preferences even politics of the day.

"Neither of us was prepared for the evening to end. When the orchestra leader announced the last dance, the one my father had saved for his own, Jonathan and I said our reluctant goodbyes. We did not foresee that it would be a long three years before we were to set eyes on each other again."

"Three years. Good grief. You don't look that old. If you had a three year wait to see him again and then…. How long was your engagement? You had a three year old when you… when you passed away? How old were you at this Ball?"

"I was fourteen, the usual age for a first formal dance."

"Wow, you were just a kid."

"I was young, yes. Still, after that night, I found it hard to think about anything other than seeing Jonathan again. Helen and Darcy at times grew weary of hearing me go on about him. My parents were mildly amused over my infatuation. My father thought I was much too young to be taken seriously. He treated me like a child since I was the youngest of my siblings.

My mother actually thought that Jonathan would be a good match for me, yet she too thought I was only captivated by my first encounter with a possible suitor. Ironically, despite her great love for my late grandfather, my grandmother believed that security rather than love should be a woman's first priority. With Jonathan's excellent position and prospects, she and my mother actually agreed on something for a change. Regardless of my family's sentiments I knew that Jonathan and I were kindred spirits."

"You're such a romantic." Holly hugged herself dramatically and blew Emeline a kiss.

Emeline cleared her throat. "You should be more respectful of your elders, young lady."

"Elders? You're kidding, right? You are probably younger than I am. Never mind. I have a sarcastic streak a mile wide. I'll try to behave."

"Good. When I learned that Jonathan's father had sent him away to England to supervise a new shipping enterprise I was disheartened. You can imagine how overjoyed I was to receive my first letter from him. There were many more to follow. As we corresponded, my affection for him deepened.

"All the while, I worked feverishly to finish my charm string. Sense or nonsense, I felt that the string had to be completed by the time Jonathan returned. Days turned to months and months to years. Still, the letters kept coming. I wrote to him every day, sending the letters in batches with small tokens of my affection.

"Finally, the day came when his ship landed in New York. Within days he finished his business at the docks thereupon he begged his father for leave to travel to Indiana."

"I kind of wish you still had that charm string. I would like to see it."

"I have not wanted to see it myself. Any reminder that I am not with Jonathan has been too painful to bear." Emeline got up from the rocker and walked toward the fireplace. She reached up to the mantle and began feeling around for something. She pulled down a bundle tied in a blue cloth.

Emeline crossed to the chaise and sat down next to Holly. She placed the package on Holly's lap. "Go ahead, open it."

Holly cautiously unwrapped the cloth bundle. Inside was a very long string of antique buttons. There were all sizes and shapes. Some were made of wood, others looked to be ivory, and still others were made from gemstones. Holly seemed fascinated with each and every one as she silently fingered them.

While Holly was busy with the button string, Emeline kept on with her history. "Nathaniel Evans was curious as to his son's interest in a young woman whom he had spent very little time with, so he decided to accompany Jonathan on the trip. When they arrived at their residence in Evansville, Jonathan wanted to see me right away.

"His father had other plans. Nathaniel Evans made his way to the bank where he requested a meeting with my father. Of course, Father could not refuse even though he had to reschedule his day to accommodate him.

"According to Father, Mr. Evans grilled him for over an hour, questioning him in regard to everything from my schooling and talents to the existence of a dowry. My father spent the evening nursing a headache; my mother didn't know whether to be flattered or offended by the interrogatory." Emeline let out a little giggle as she recalled her parents' reactions to Mr. Evans' scrutiny.

"The next day Jonathan and his father showed up at our doorstep unannounced. Our housekeeper, Gertrude, let them in and escorted them to Mother's parlor to wait for us.

"I was in my room, and Mother was in the kitchen with Marianne when they arrived. Gertrude scurried through the kitchen doors informing Mother that she had guests. There was much rushing about to prepare tea and cakes.

"To fetch me, Mother tiptoed up the back stairs. I spent a few moments fussing with my hair while I peered into the looking glass above my dressing table. I was so nervous and anxious to see Jonathan that I almost lost my balance on the stairs. Luckily I did not tumble down them in a heap.

"As soon as our eyes met I knew that all would be well. Jonathan rose from the settee and met us as we walked through the parlor door. He took my hand and kissed it, he told me how wonderful it was to see me again. Mr. Evans also rose from his seat, but did not approach us. After greetings had been exchanged, Mother and I sat on the divan facing the men. Jonathan returned to his seat as they too sat down.

"Marianne arrived with the tea cart, and thereupon everyone was served. Mr. Evans asked a lot of questions, just as he had done with Father at the bank. It was obvious that he was interviewing me and my family, assessing our worthiness as in-laws.

"Jonathan was noticeably embarrassed by his father's behavior. He tried to lighten the mood by changing the subject; He related humorous anecdotes about his time in England. When we had all finished our tea, Mr. Evans seemed satisfied with our responses to his interrogation, so they said their good-byes. Gertrude presented them with their coats."

Emeline wasn't sure how much of her story Holly was absorbing because the button chain continued to hold her attention. Holly carefully examined each button. Emeline had to concede that they *were* astonishingly beautiful. Each and every one was unique. Whether Holly was hearing her or not, Emeline had to divulge her secrets.

"Several days went by without a word from either Jonathan or his father. My appetite left me, sleep eluded me. Mother fussed about, unsure as to how to go about comforting me. I busied myself by completing my button chain with a large handful of buttons given to me by my grandmother. She was as determined as I was that the chain be finished.

"One day a messenger arrived. Jonathan had been called back to New York on urgent business, but he would be back midmonth. He asked to call on me when he returned. I was of course delighted that he had not forgotten me, but disappointed that it would be so long until I saw him again. I counted the days until he finally sent word that he was on his way back to Evansville.

"When he appeared on our doorstep, he brought flowers for me as well as sweets for Mother. Our courtship was brief; he held to the propriety expected of him, yet we both knew that it was merely a formality. That spring Jonathan proposed marriage on a moonlight stroll through Mother's garden."

Emeline held her hands over her heart and let out a heavy sigh. The dramatic gesture did not escape Holly's notice even if she was somewhat distracted by the amazing button chain.

"You're a bit of a drama queen." Holly mimed Emeline's gesture holding her hands over her chest and heaving theatrically. She laughed. "I'm sorry but it's hard to take you seriously when you do stuff like that."

"You have obviously never been in love. Hopefully one day you too will experience the joy that true love brings." Emeline hefted her skirts from the settee and stood. She gave Holly a fretful look and walked to the fireplace where she stared into the blaze as she spoke.

"When Jonathan proposed, at that moment, my heart felt as though it would burst with love for him. I rushed impetuously to accept his offer, but he stopped me mid-sentence with a qualifier.

"If I were to marry him, I had to agree to follow him on his venture out west. He said he was serious about leaving his father's business. He was ready to set out for the Territories. Not only had he studied the ranching business, he had also purchased cattle and made arrangements for their transport. A friend had tipped him off about a place near the Mexican border where we might homestead a piece of land with mountains and wide open spaces.

"Jonathan's enthusiasm for this course of action was contagious. Enticed by the romance of his plan, I agreed, and a plot was hatched.

"Indubitably neither of our families would have approved of our plans. My mother began to design a grand wedding; Father strutted around as proud as a peacock. I simply could not tell them anything as much as my heart ached to do so. I had sworn an oath to Jonathan that I would not say a word.

"We conspired to elope, and then send a message back to them as soon as we were well on our way out west. I kept our secret for weeks as Jonathan finalized his plans and collected supplies to have shipped ahead. I played along with Mother's arrangements, yet I remained detached enough to appear flighty, unable to choose between color schemes, fabrics and menus.

"I did not want her to place orders or reservations that could not be cancelled. Despite her obvious frustration with me, she kept her patience. She attributed my behavior to a case of the nerves."

Emeline turned to face Holly, who seemed to be more attentive than she had been. Emeline was pleased. "My grandmother sensed that something was afoot. She had an uncanny way of knowing what to expect before it happened, and she could discern deception of any sort. Granting that it had been a while since she and I had engaged in much meaningful conversation, she began to look askance at my comportment.

"She was, however, somewhat distracted, still in mourning for my grandfather even though it was well over a year since the accident. He had died from injuries sustained at the steel mill, the factory where he had both amassed a fortune and, sadly, lost his life.

"Grandmother was often sullen; she would keep to herself or take jaunts to the graveyard where she would visit with Grandfather. During the year following his death, she had kept a small glass vial, her tear catcher, in a satin pouch which hung from her belt next to her chatelaine.

"Each time she wept for her husband, she would collect the tears. On the anniversary of his death, she poured them out upon his grave. Even after her period of mourning she still wore the vial along with the black mourning clothes that had become her daily costume." Emeline was saddened by the memory of her grandmother and it shone on her face.

"If Grandmother had her suspicions, she managed to keep them to herself. One Saturday afternoon about a month after Jonathan proposed he came to the house, driving the motor car that his father had purchased for him as a wedding gift. He spoke with my father; he asked if he might take me to his parent's home for dinner.

"At first my father was taken aback by the impromptu invitation, but because I was Jonathan's fiancé he agreed to the request, providing I would have a proper escort home at a reasonable hour. Jonathan assured Father that all would be well and we left the house.

"Unbeknownst to anyone save Jonathan and I, I had stowed a trunk full of my belongings in a shed which sat at the back side of Aunt Vivienne's property. We rode around the block, and stopped just long enough for Jonathan to slip in the back gate, and retrieve the small trunk. Without delay we were off to start our lives together."

"So there is a rebel hiding under all of that heavy clothing and stuffy language." Holly grinned at Emeline, who ignored the comment and kept going.

"Jonathan had a dear chum named Thomas. The two had been friends since early childhood. Thomas's father was a judge, which meant that he could perform our nuptials. The good judge was also a friend of my father's so although he agreed to perform the marriage rite, he did not promise to be silent in the matter. We knew that it would be only a matter of time before both my parents and Jonathan's were made aware of our treachery."

Emeline suddenly went silent; she seemed to be studying the lace on the edge of her shirtsleeve. Holly cleared her throat. Emeline looked up, she locked eyes with Holly. "I know what you must think of us. We never meant to hurt anyone nor disrespect our families."

Holly started to respond, "No, I wasn't thinking...."

Emeline cut her off with a heavy sigh of relief. Then she continued. "I realize you must be weary of listening to me by now, so I will hasten my story.

"After a night in a country inn, a long ride to the train station and countless cities along the line, Jonathan and I finally made it to the Territories. In Silver City, we picked up the horses as well as the livery. Next, we met up with the cowboys who drove our cattle from Texas.

"We camped out for the first time. We rode our first buckboard with a pair of mules to pull it over rocky desert trails. The wide-open space and tall mountains were nothing like the rolling green landscape of home. We came to love our new home just as we loved each other. We were truly blessed.

"The land that we were to homestead laid at the foot of a high mountain range amid a forest of pine, oak, fir, and sycamore. There was much work to do in the beginning. Our saving grace came from our nearest neighbor, Mr. Eastwood.

"He was an experienced rancher, a homesteader. A widower with a fifteen-year-old son, he was more than happy to trade his building and cattle raising skills for my cooking, cleaning, and mending. Jonathan also gave Jeb Eastwood financial advice when he inherited a large sum of money from his late wife's estate.

"The first months after we arrived at the property were difficult; I would be lying if I told you that I was not homesick. Life was harsh, dirty, at times miserable, yet only physically. Emotionally, I was still so excited to be Jonathan's wife that I could have endured most anything. I know that he felt the same way because he told me so every day.

"Soon after the house was built, a well dug and the windmill erected, I learned that I was expecting a child. Nothing could have made us happier. We anxiously awaited your arrival."

Holly squirmed around on the chaise, a troubled look on her face. Emeline knew that Holly was uncomfortable with the idea that she had once been Emeline's child. Still, there was no doubt in Emeline's mind, and Holly would have to accept the fact sooner rather than later.

"I missed my Mother very much during those many days. We had not heard directly from home, but Jonathan's brother sent a telegram, he told us that both sets of parents seemed to react to our elopement in a similar manner. First there was shock and disbelief, then anger. Ultimately, after a while, they appeared to have accepted the fact much as people eventually accept the death of a loved one.

"I yearned to speak with them, and Jonathan was in agreement, yet he wanted to wait until our child was born. He felt that the news of a grandchild would cushion the inevitably uncomfortable communication.

Finally, the day came. You were born early Christmas Eve morning, with only your father in attendance. There were no doctors or midwives close by. Mother would have been mortified. Nonetheless, you were healthy, perfect in every way. We named you Ivy for the beautiful greens that were always hung about the house during the holidays back home in Indiana.

Holly was now sitting up straight with her eyes watching Emeline intently. Emeline smiled at her, pleased to have the full attention of her audience.

"We were gloriously happy. Jonathan rode into town a few days later to send a telegraph to our families. As he anticipated, he had answers back the next time he made the trip for supplies. After that, we received letters and even packages with gifts for you, along with many pleas for us to return to Indiana and civilization. Our replies were kind but firm in our desire to remain on our ranch in the wilderness.

"Swiftly the years passed. You had your third birthday. I made you a small cake and a new dress from one of my own that I cut up for the fabric. You were a very happy child, full of life and abundant curiosity. You worshiped your father as did I, and of course he reciprocated. There was nothing he could deny you. This was why you went to look for him that fateful evening."

Holly leaned forward as Emeline turned toward the door, her head down.

"It was just past supper time, I was still washing up. You became bored and began to beg me to allow you to play outside. I told you to stay in the side yard, though I should have known that you would go looking for Jonathan. He was down near the creek chopping firewood.

When I realized that you were gone, I went to look for you. A summer monsoon storm had rolled in, bringing gusty winds, thunder, lightning, and rain. You were too close to the creek when the flash flood waters rushed toward you.

Initially, Jonathan and I were too far away to snatch you from the torrent, but as soon as he saw you in the water, he was moving, running toward the creek. Without thinking, he leapt into the current still carrying a load of logs strapped to his body. You were both fighting the roaring water as I stood watching, helpless, screaming. In an instant, you were both gone from sight, and I was left to mourn."

Holly gulped for air. Emeline rushed to the chaise. "Are you alright?"

"I'm okay, I just didn't expect… I mean I didn't realize…." Holly was tearing up.

"Let me finish, I have to tell you the rest." Emeline patted Holly on the shoulder. "Mr. Eastwood found your bodies the following day. He and his son helped me to bury you both on the small hillside behind the house. In the first months he came by to check on me daily, he brought food and supplies from town, he even made me an offer of marriage.

"I turned him down, of course, because Jonathan was my one and only love. I believe that I must have suffered a breakdown because I recollect very little after the tragedy. I had no appetite; I could not sleep. I spent my days and nights sitting or lying near your graves. I developed a bad cough; my hair began to fall out, my skin became ashen.

"My death may have been attributed to exposure, starvation, or disease, though I know that the genuine cause was grief, my shattered heart.

"The night it happened, the night I died, I was on the hillside as usual. It was hours past twilight, and cold. I lay curled up near the small crosses that Jeb had fashioned to mark your final resting places. I had no tears left, so I merely whimpered. Something drew my eye, a pinpoint of light in the sky above me. I thought it was a star.

"As I gazed into the heavens, the light began to grow both in size and intensity. I heard female voices calling my name. I thought that it must be angels.

"I closed my eyes and held fast to the brass locket that Jonathan had given to me. The locket held photographs of all three of us. A traveling man with a camera had taken them when we were in town just a few months before your death. I added locks of your hair and Jonathan's after you passed.

"I didn't hear your voices or see your faces. I was confused. I wanted more than anything to join you and your father. I was convinced that you had crossed into the afterlife. My grandmother spoke often of Heaven, almost as often as Parson Williams, our minister back in Indiana.

"The female voices became insistent, the light brighter. I recoiled, hiding my eyes, I held ever tighter to the locket. Suddenly the voices ceased, cold blackness surrounded me. I was petrified, I wondered if I was destined for Hell. I wished with all my might that I might return to the safety of the ranch. Time seemed to stand still. I lay there curled up tight, wishing, shivering in the cold night.

"Suddenly something changed. Even though my eyes were still shut I could see glimmers of light, I began to feel warmer, more comfortable. I cautiously opened my eyes slowly focusing on my surroundings. I was no longer on the hill, no longer outside, I was here in this room, this house, our house, Hideaway Ranch. I have tried to leave, to simply walk out the door but I cannot."

Emeline stood before Holly at the conclusion of her tale, waiting for a response. She quietly moved to sit next to the woman who was once her little girl.

Holly shifted in her seat. "I'm trying to process everything. It seems to be more than a coincidence that Ivy and I share a birthday, not to mention we were both named for Christmastime plants." She paused.

"I don't think there is any way that I could be imagining all of this, so I guess you must be real and your elaborate story must be true - or at least you believe it's true.

"I feel so bad for you. How awful it must be to lose your family like that. I lost my parents in an accident, so I do understand your grief." Holly put her arm around Emeline's shoulders.

Emeline leaned into Holly's embrace, her hands nervously straightening her clothing.

"The lace on your dress and veil is beautiful," Holly whispered. "Is that the dress you were wearing when you, um, passed on?"

"Oh, no. I would have had to have ordered the fabric to sew the dress myself or I would have had to go to town and order a mourning dress. I was in no condition to do either.

"I was wearing one of my simple linen frocks that I wore almost daily. I brought only two of my nicest gowns with me when we left Indiana and I wore them only for special occasions. This ensemble that I have on was what I wished for when I ended up here." Emeline made a sweeping gesture around the room.

"I don't know what to say. It's beautiful, but maybe you should think about wishing for a new outfit, something more colorful."

"I will not end my mourning until I am reunited with Jonathan." Emeline sounded firm.

"For your sake, I hope that happens. I'm not sure it's safe to stay here in this illusion, or whatever it really is. I'm a little worried, too, about our collective sanity. I have a million questions for you, but they can wait."

Emeline sobbed and reached into the hidden pocket inside her sleeve for a hanky to wipe her eyes. Holly still had her arm around Emeline. She gave her another squeeze and sniffled as she fought back her own sorrow.

Chapter Seven

Joseph slowly roused from the vivid dream that held a grip on his unconscious mind. In the dream, he had stood in front of a mirror, his reflection gazing back at him. Beyond the reflection, a filmy curtain waved in an illusionary breeze that he could not feel. Shadows moved behind the curtain and women's voices seemed to be coming from inside the mirror. In the nightmare, Joseph turned around to see if this curtain and the figures beyond were actually behind him or if they were somehow inside the mirror itself. When he turned to look, they were not there.

His common sense, even in the dream, told him that it was not possible for people or objects to reside in a mirror, but his eyes and ears told another story. He strained to hear what the voices were saying. Leaning in closer he still couldn't make out the words, only the tone, which seemed argumentative.

As the vision faded, he woke feeling irritated; Joseph hated leaving matters unresolved even if it was only a dream. His head and neck ached from being held at such an awkward angle for so long. That's what he deserved for falling asleep sitting up, he thought as he stretched. Regaining his wits, it dawned on him that he was still in his darkroom. "Oh no! My photos!"

As he looked at his wristwatch, he was startled by the loud beep... beep... beep of the timer as it went off. Could it be that he had only been asleep for twenty-five minutes? It felt as if had been hours. He double-checked the time to be sure. Remarkably, it was true. "Wow! Thank God."

He breathed a heavy sigh. It would have been devastating to lose all of those amazing shots. Quickly, he used a squeegee to remove the excess photoflow, removed the prints, and then hung them in the drying tank. He used hanging clips on both ends. It would take at least an hour for them to dry. In the meantime, he would prepare for the final phase of the process.

Joseph's house had a very open floor plan, much like his nonna's. He left the large walk-in closet that served as his darkroom and strode through his bedroom into the main part of the house. The living room sat to his left; the dining room and kitchen were straight ahead. A half wall separated the living area from the kitchen. On the dining room table lay a pile of books, a couple of camera lenses, a full key ring, and a handful of change.

Beginning with the books, Joseph began to clear everything off the table. When nothing was left other than the tablecloth, he removed that too. He piled all the items onto the top of a low bookcase that sat just inside the dining area. He would deal with it later. A long buffet stood on an adjacent wall. From the top drawer, he pulled a clean tablecloth and draped it across the surface of the table. Here, he would bring the dry film, lay it flat with the shiny side down, cut it apart; then, lastly, he would place the prints in acetate sleeves.

With that preparatory task accomplished, Joseph realized that he was starving. *That's the problem with pasta. It just doesn't stick with me for long.* He headed to the kitchen to find a snack. As he did so, he glanced at the wall clock above the stove. Sophie would be up by now, getting ready for work. Once he grabbed a bite to eat, he needed to give her a call.

He stood in front of the open refrigerator door mulling over the choices. There certainly wasn't much to choose from. It occurred to him that a trip to the grocery store was unavoidable. Joseph loved to cook and he was a capable chef. He just wasn't crazy about making lists or shopping for the ingredients.

He reached in for the last of the bread as well as the nearly empty peanut butter jar. There was a jar of honey in the pantry. Gathering the ingredients, he crafted a sandwich. Regretting the lack of milk in the house, he dispensed himself a glass of water from the fridge before he sat down in his favorite chair to eat.

The house seemed unusually quiet. Maybe he would turn on the tube for a few minutes. The remote sat on the end table where he had left it last. After a few minutes of channel surfing, he decided to turn it off. Somewhere in the back of his mind, he knew that what he was doing was a feeble attempt to fill time, to keep from thinking about the girl, his Lois Lane.

He worried about her. *What if she doesn't make it? I would feel guilty; even though I know I did all I could have done for her. She'll be fine. After all, she is breathing on her own. But... maybe she has internal injuries. I have to call Sophie. All of this speculation has to end. Once I know that she is going to recover, I'll be able to stop thinking about her. At least I hope so.*

Now, where did I leave my phone? Damn, I think I left it in the Jeep. I wonder how many calls I've missed. When he opened the front door, the sun temporarily blinded him. It was a beautiful day, too nice to be cooped up indoors. *After I call Sophie, maybe I'll head over to the park; take a few shots of the sunset.* The park had some rolling hills, and the view from a particular hilltop made for perfect 'end of day' photos.

Joseph opened the driver's-side door. There in the console he saw his cell sitting right where he had left it. Shaking his head at his forgetfulness, he grabbed the phone, turned around and stepped back inside the house to avoid the glare. He pressed the icon for Sophie at the top of his home screen. She answered on the third ring.

"Hi Joseph, what's shaking?"

"I just wanted to catch you before you left for work."

"Too late. I just arrived. I'm in the parking lot. There are two temps working tonight. I thought I'd better come in a little early to show them around before report."

"Oh, well ... I was hoping you could do me that favor. Could you check on the girl from Turkey Creek for me?"

"Yeah. I remembered, but you know I can't tell you any details about her condition or anything. All I can do is check to see if she has been identified and let you know if she can have visitors."

"I know, confidentiality. Got it. Really, I just want to know that she's going to be okay."

"Sure, I can understand that. I'll call you back in a little while."

"Great. Later."

"Later."

I guess I'll check on those negatives. Joseph wandered into his bedroom. He lifted the heavy curtain that separated his sleeping quarters from his darkroom. He opened the drying cabinet and examined the prints. They looked dry, so he removed and carefully stacked them for transport to the dining room table.

He laid the large sheets out and cut them apart into the desired sizes, and then he slipped the finished photos into protective sleeves. He was proud of his work. The colors and angles were stunning. Smiling, Joseph began to pack his camera gear into travel bags. With nothing but the park and the promise of twilight on his mind, he left the house. Once his gear was loaded into the rear of the Jeep, he buckled up and was about to pull out of the driveway when his phone sounded a familiar ringtone.

"Wow. That was fast, Sophie. Did you find out anything?"

"I did indeed. Her name is Holly Marie Montgomery. I can't give you anything personal like her age or her measurements." Sophie just had to give him a bit of ribbing.

"You're hilarious Soph. Anything else that you *can* tell me? Like how she is doing and if I can take her the necklace?" Nonna had filled Sophie in on the locket.

"Her condition is listed as stable. You can take her the necklace, but I think she might still be under sedation. You should wait until after eight o'clock, after dinner and shift change."

"Thanks for the report. I guess I'll wait until tomorrow. Talk to you later."

"All right Joseph. Bye."

Joseph tossed his phone into the console and leaned back in his seat. He ran the young woman's name through his mind committing it to memory. Holly Marie Montgomery. Holly. It was a nice name, not terribly common. He thought the name fit her, though he didn't even know her.

Being in a "stable" condition was a good thing he supposed. That meant she wasn't likely to die. He hoped she would make a full recovery. It was so exasperating not to be able to see her, return the locket and put this whole thing behind him.

The park was crowded. Joseph saw groups of kids, with adults trying to corral them. He realized that there must be a team sign-up going on. The quiet nature shots he had hoped to get would have to wait. He sat in the Jeep at the side of the road debating what to do next. *I could go home and work on the digital photos. There is a lot of work to do there. Or I could meet up with everybody earlier than planned.* His friends had invited him to join them for dinner and drinks later.

Finally, he knew what he had to do first. *Hell, I'll go to the hospital, and take my chances.* His watch said it was seven-oh-seven.

Chapter Eight

Joseph's nonna, his grandmother, Rosa Romero was just waking from a long nap. Her arthritis pain signaled her that she had slept long enough. It was time to get up and take her medication. Slowly she rose to sit, swinging her legs carefully over the edge of the bed.

Rosa didn't mind getting older; she just hated being old. It slowed her down. The family had always relied on Rosa; she could get a job done. She wasn't ready to give that up. Aches and pains be damned. She would press on.

Slipping her feet into her fuzzy house shoes Rosa shuffled into the kitchen. Her pain medication sat on the counter to the right of the sink. She took a glass from the dish drainer and turned on the tap. Filling the glass with a little water, she opened the pill bottle, emptied two tablets into her left hand, and then popped them into her mouth, chasing them down with the water.

As she tilted her head back slightly to take the pills, she spotted out of the corner of her eye the locket lying on the table where Joseph had left it.

Remembering that she had promised to clean it, she opened the cabinet under the sink to look through her assortment of cleaning products. She chose a bottle of jewelry cleaner along with a small basket-full of brushes and rags, moistened some of the cloths with water, and then walked over to the table. The locket was cleaner now than it had been when Joseph found it. Some of the mud had dried and rubbed or flaked off from riding around in his pocket.

Rosa turned it over in her hand. She began cleaning it by using a soft brush to remove the crusted mud from the edges. As she came to the clasp, she flicked it with her thumb. The locket fell open showing a muddied interior.

Although the pages unfolded, the photos inside were practically impossible to see clearly through the dirty glass. She carefully dabbed at the surfaces with a damp cloth.

The old photographs inside the oval frames were barely recognizable. Rosa could make out that one was a gentleman, the other a little girl, both in nineteenth century clothing. The two inner pages held woven strands of hair. She recognized the piece as being a memorial keepsake.

The tiny pieces of glass that protected each of the photos as well as the locks of hair were difficult to remove. Rosa rose from her seat and walked over to the kitchen. She pulled out the top drawer where she kept an assortment of tools, gadgets, and other odds and ends. She found the tweezers she was looking for, but as she started to close the drawer, something else caught her eye.

A deck of playing cards in a plastic case lay at the front of the drawer. She picked them up and carried them to the table along with the tweezers and a handful of other tools she thought she might need to finish cleaning the locket.

After some careful dabbing, wiping and polishing the locket looked almost as good as it had when Holly first tidied it up herself. Rosa admired the elaborate floral design on the cover. As she held the open pendant in her hand, a feeling of sorrow came over her. More than sadness or pity for the person who once owned this necklace, this emotion was akin to despair.

Tears fell in rivulets down Rosa's well-lined face. She closed the locket setting it down on the table. Rosa began to pray. "San Michele to the right of me; San Michele to the left of me. San Michele above me; San Michele below me. San Michele within me; San Michele all around me. San Michele, with your flaming sword of cobalt blue, please protect me. Amen."

Ending her prayer, Rosa crossed herself and took up the cards. Though the Romero family was Roman Catholic through and through, Rosa's family, the Andaloros, came from a rural region of Southern Italy. In their small village, old folk traditions and the Catholic faith were married.

While the Church frowned on such practices as fortune telling, charm making, and the worship of ancestral spirits, Rosa reconciled the old ways to the new in her own religious practice. She came from a long line of women with "the sight."

Rosa herself was not as gifted as her mother before her. Her mother had profound visions, peering into the future with uncanny accuracy. Rosa had intuitive dreams, plus she could read people's energy well, but self-doubt prevented her from achieving her mother's success in the art of divination.

Rosa removed the cards from their box. She began to shuffle them thoroughly, cutting the deck and re-shuffling until she was mentally ready to proceed. She lay ten cards in a cross pattern on the table in front of her while she concentrated on Joseph, the young woman and the locket. She read each card as she placed it down:

- The Jack of hearts - Joseph
- The five of hearts – His mind clouded with indecision.
- Two cards stuck together. Two Queens, odd. The Queen of Hearts as well as the Queen of Clubs. Both Queens are faithful companions. Why two cards?
- The four of Spades – Misfortune, illness. Could that be the young woman in the hospital?
- The four of Clubs – Danger. Supposed friends, one turning against the other.
- The Ace of Clubs – A good card. It points to Joseph's popularity. Everyone loves Joseph.
- The Three of Clubs - Multiple marriage. What might that mean?
- The three of Spades reversed - A bewildering situation or confused mind.
- The two of Spades - Complete and forced change. A sudden change of location, relationship - or a death. Bound to make a big difference in the coming months.

What did this mean for Joseph? The reading wasn't overtly negative. It was, however, troubling. Rosa picked up the locket. As she opened it, she held it in her left palm. Next, she rested her right hand over the top of the card layout and bowed her head. Rosa then did something only her oldest daughter had ever witnessed: she went into a deep trance. She began by relaxing her entire body. She leaned forward, resting her head on the table. Next, she posed her question. "Show me your secrets," she stated out loud to the locket.

Her senses began to heighten. First her sense of smell, followed immediately by taste. She smelled wood smoke, tasted the charcoal; ensuingly she inhaled a whiff of freshly baked cookies, tasting the butter and sugar. Lastly, a fresh floral perfume permeated the air. Although the smell was sweet, it left a bitter taste in her mouth.

Rosa began to twitch, her muscles in spasm as though she were convulsing. She heard voices, the click of a latch, the creak of a door hinge.

The blackness behind her closed eyelids vanished. She found herself standing in front of a large oval mirror. On the other side of the glass stood two women, staring at her. Their eyes were wide with either fear or amazement. Rosa startled, but remained in her trance. She studied the young women.

One was a fresh-faced brunette with a smattering of freckles across the bridge of her nose, and bright blue eyes. She wore a pair of shorts with a tank top.

The other young lady was dressed all in black, a long nineteenth-century dress; on her head she wore a cap with a veil attached. Her blond hair was pinned up, with a few long strands escaping to frame her face. Her eyes were a rare shade of violet blue. Her features were small, delicate. She was a good six inches shorter than the brunette.

They were an odd pair. Both were beautiful girls, yet very different. As Rosa pondered, the women began to talk to each other. Rosa struggled to hear the conversation. She heard the words "a way out." The women turned back to the glass, reached out to touch it…. Together they shouted, "Help us!"

Rosa's heart skipped a beat. Her head snapped forward, banging on the table. Pain was the catalyst that brought her back to consciousness. She was dizzy at first; she braced herself on the table with her elbows as she slowly sat upright. The temperature in the room had dropped, causing Rosa to break out in goose bumps from head to toe. The hair on the back of her arms and the nape of her neck stood on end. Her pulse was racing.

She still didn't understand exactly what was going on with the locket. Her question hadn't been answered in any clear way, though in her estimation, the thing was haunted. She didn't want Joseph to have it in his possession.

Rising from the table, the locket clutched in her hand, she felt a little shaky, so she leaned on the table for a few minutes until she regained her strength. Food would be necessary; she always needed to eat something after leaving the dream state of trance. She didn't do this often, thank goodness. It took a lot out of her, especially now that she was older.

Before she fixed herself a light supper, she wanted to put the locket somewhere safe. She walked through the living room into the hallway that led to her bedroom. In a small alcove sat a three-tiered shelf. On the top shelf were three statues. In the center, Mary the Blessed Virgin. To her left the effigy of a three faced woman, the Parcae or Fates. On her right was a statue handmade by Rosa herself to represent the Lare, the ancestor Spirits whose job it was to watch over the family. Above the shelf, hanging on the wall was a framed print of Jesus on the cross. Rosa crossed herself, and then placed the locket on the shelf at the feet of the Fates.

Now she could get something to eat, and maybe watch one of her favorite shows before trying to sleep. In the kitchen, she decided that she was in the mood for a pizza. Her own homemade pizza was a staple at family gatherings. This night she reached for the phone placing an order for delivery. One local pizzeria made a pretty decent pie. She stood with the phone in her hand.

I wonder if I ought to call Joseph, fill him in on my vision. I don't know … Joseph is a college graduate and a man of science. Hmm, well, it can't hurt to try. He might listen, and maybe something I say will influence him to return the locket as soon as possible and leave well enough alone.

Joseph's phone rang and rang, finally going to his voicemail. Rosa hated leaving messages; she didn't like talking to a machine. "Joseph, this is Nonna. I need to talk to you about this locket. I did a reading. I think it is cursed. I know that sounds crazy, but you need to give this thing back. Walk away. I'm serious. Call me when you get this message. I love you, Tesoro."

Hopefully he will get the message tonight. May the grace of God rid him of this malocchio, this curse. Rosa called the pizza joint, and then sat down in her recliner to wait. She turned on the TV, doing her best to lose herself in the mindless entertainment before her.

Chapter Nine

Joseph had a run of luck and hit almost all green lights on his way to the hospital. He even managed to score a decent parking place. Feeling pretty good, he bounded up the steps to the front entrance and breezed into the lobby along with a group of people carrying flowers and gifts.

From the gift-wrap and the large Mylar balloon proclaiming **IT'S A GIRL!** he gathered that someone had just had a baby. He smiled and nodded at the group "Congrats." A chorus of "Thanks" came in reply.

At the elevator, Joseph attempted to recall the layout of the hospital. He visited Sophie at work on occasion, and he thought he knew where the ICU was located, so he proceeded in that direction. The hall of the unit was bustling with activity. Joseph walked past a group of nurses, and though they turned to look at him as he passed, they didn't question him.

Glancing at the board posted on the wall behind the nurse's station, he saw Holly's room number. He had no trouble locating it, and cautiously stepped into her small room with his eyes trained on the figure lying beneath a blue blanket with "Lumberjacks" embroidered in the corner. At first glance, Joseph was sure he had the wrong room. Although her head was turned to one side, the long blond curls that fell across the pillow were not the shoulder-length locks of the woman he rescued from the creek.

Joseph backed up and took another look at the room number outside the door; he confirmed that the number was correct. Once again he moved into the room. This time as he approached the bed, he saw the honey brown hair he remembered. His eyes must have been playing tricks on him.

He walked over to Holly's bedside and looked down at her sleeping form. She was hooked up to monitors and tubes. That was to be expected, but still the sight pained him. He had hoped to find her drowsy, but not in this comatose state, completely unaware of his presence.

There was a chair in the corner of the room. He moved it to the side of the bed and sat down. Holly's hair covered her face, so he gently brushed it back. He reached for her hand, and held it between his. She looked peaceful, innocent. Joseph felt that protective urge come over him. Something about this woman brought out an almost fatherly instinct in Joseph that he had a hard time understanding.

She was no child, probably a few years his junior. He had dated younger women without feeling a fatherly need to safeguard them in the way he did Holly. He sat there just looking at her for several minutes.

He studied her face again the way he had on the evening of the accident. She was lovely, even in the non-flattering lighting of the hospital. Her skin was glowing with a golden even tone, though he knew she wore no make-up. Joseph couldn't take his eyes off her.

As he sat there in his reverie, she began to stir. Her body jerked. Behind her closed eyelids, her eyes were twitching. A mewling noise escaped her throat, though her lips remained just slightly parted in a half smile. Joseph wasn't sure if he should be concerned. No alarms were going off, and the monitors beside her bed beeped at a steady rate with a regular pattern displayed on the screen.

He concluded that she must be having a dream. Rising from the chair, he leaned over her and whispered in her ear "Don't worry; I'm here for you Holly." Without thinking, he began to croon.

"Lazily, easily, swings now the wheel round. Slowly and lowly is heard now the reel's sound. Noiseless and light to the lattice above her, the maid steps, then leaps to the arms of her lover.

"Merrily, cheerily, noiselessly whirring, swings the wheel, spins the wheel while the foot's stirring.

Spritely and lightly and merrily ringing, trills the sweet voice of the young maiden singing."

Holly seemed to react to the song. As she relaxed, her breathing slowed. Joseph eased back into the chair beside her, resting his forehead in his hands.

What was happening to him, he wondered. That old song was back, and somehow his mind related it to this perfect stranger.

The tune itself was an enigma. No one in his family claimed to have taught it to him. As Nonna told it, one day when he was three years old, he just started singing it to himself at naptime. Everyone assumed that he learned it from TV. He didn't think so.

Joseph again reached for Holly's hand; he relaxed in the chair, losing track of time as he drifted off in thought. Suddenly he was startled by a familiar sound. It sounded like the chimes of a grandfather clock. How odd, he thought as he blinked his eyes in disbelief. Looking around him, he was no longer in the hospital with Holly.

The chair he sat on was now a settee, and he found himself inside a stately drawing room, seated next to a beautiful, graceful blond woman dressed in Victorian clothing, who was smiling sweetly at him. He knew her, he loved her; but at the same time, he could not bring to mind her name. Why was he fantasizing about this other woman when he sat at the bedside of the woman he was doubtless falling for?

Just as he had that thought, the hallucination ended. He was back in Holly's hospital room, still seated in the chair next to her bed. Joseph determined that he must be overtired. It was at that moment that he remembered why he came in the first place... the locket.

Oh man, I can't believe it. I left that damn thing at Nonna's. I guess I'll have to come back. Smiling to himself, Joseph leaned over and kissed the top of Holly's head. "I'll see you later, sleeping beauty."

A feeling of bliss washed over Joseph as he returned the chair to the corner. He glanced back at Holly before reluctantly leaving the room. This was not like anything else he had ever experienced.

Chapter Ten

Scattered clouds filtered the rising sun as it peeked over the ridge of the Chiricahua mountain range. A light breeze danced through the leaves of the desert willows that bordered the south side of the Nolans' front yard. Birds of various colors and sizes were drawn to the bird feeders that had been placed around the terraced desert landscape. A vivid red Vermillion Flycatcher stood out, though the brightly colored male Orioles with their yellow-orange hues rivaled his chromatic beauty.

Last night's storm had been plenteous. The rain gauge that hung from the fence post measured over an inch of rain, which was a lot for one storm considering the total amount of rainfall during a typical monsoon season was usually six to eight inches. The morning was cool, comfortable with the temperature in the low to mid seventies. The high was projected to be in the nineties. Anything that needed done outside would have to get done before the heat set in.

Dottie Nolan sat on the patio nervously waiting for her husband Harry to return from his trek up to their rental trailers, which sat on a slope about three hundred yards north of the house. His mission was to check on Holly, their summer tenant. The young woman, whom Dottie had come to think of as another daughter, hadn't shown up for a farewell supper last evening, nor had she stopped in this morning to say goodbye as planned. She was supposed to leave for her home in Flagstaff today.

Holly wasn't the type to blow off plans or leave without notice. Dottie had wanted to call the sheriff's office last night, but Harry told her to wait until morning, because he thought that maybe Holly had spent the night in the Forest Service cabin rather than traverse the road down the mountain in the storm.

When Dottie saw Harry coming back to the house alone, she rushed to meet him on the road. "What's going on? Is she okay?"

"She's not there. Neither is her truck. I went on in to have a look, and her clothes, books … everything is still there. It seems like she just started packing. I don't think she came back at all yesterday after she left to finish at the ranch. We need to make some calls."

After placing a call to the local sheriff's department and agreeing to wait for an officer to get back to them, Dottie went into the kitchen. She found the address book where she had written Cassie's number. Holly had described her roommate and spoke about their close relationship to the Nolans. Dottie knew that if anyone had heard from Holly it would have been Cassie. The phone rang several times before Cassie's weary voice whispered "Hello?"

"Hello, this is Dottie Nolan, may I speak with Cassie?"

"Oh, my gods, Mrs. Nolan, this is Cassie. I'm so sorry. I meant to call you before now. I feel terrible. You must be frantic about Holly. The sheriff called me last night, so I drove down. She was caught in a flash flood leaving the ranch yesterday afternoon. Some guy spotted her truck and pulled her out.

"She's in the hospital in Tucson - UMC - but the doctor says he doesn't see any reason that she won't make a full recovery. She has a concussion as well as some other bumps and bruises, but no fractures. She didn't take in much water, so her lungs are clear. They have her on fluids and antibiotics. The doctor has been keeping her sedated, watching for swelling because of the bump she took on her head. It's just precautionary.

"I'll give you her room number if you want to visit. You might want to wait until she is alert. I think the doctor was going to start gradually bringing her around later today or tomorrow. I'm in Tucson, staying at a motel near the hospital. I'll call you later with an update." Cassie blurted all of this with scarcely a breath.

"My heavens! I was afraid something bad had happened when she didn't show up for dinner last night."

Harry stood in front of Dottie making motions indicating that he wanted to be included in the conversation. "Thank you for filling us in Cassie. I'm going to pass this on to Harry. We will wait to hear back from you when you have more news."

"I will call; again, I apologize for not notifying you."

"We understand. I'm sure you have been overwhelmed by this. Holly talks about you all the time. We know you are like a sister to her."

"Yes, she is like a sister. I'm so glad that my parents asked me to take over as Holly's power of attorney when I turned twenty-one. That was necessary for me to sign all the forms for her.

"My parents are out of the country right now on a much needed vacation. I haven't been able to tell them about the accident because of the time difference. I know they will want to come home early, though I know Holly wouldn't want them to cut their trip short. I'm going to have them speak directly to the doctor."

"I think you are handling this very well. Holly was right when she said you were a strong person. She said that she relied on you, that you were always there for her."

"Wow, she really said that? I guess I have to live up to her high expectations of me." Cassie laughed and cried a little at the same time. Holly just had to be all right.

The women said their good-byes. Dottie relayed the details to Harry.

"Gee, I wonder where she got stuck." Harry sat down at the kitchen table. Taking off his hat, he fanned himself with it. "It sounds as though she was really lucky. There usually aren't too many folks out and about up there, especially during a storm. I wonder who this fella was that pulled our girl to safety. I'd like to shake his hand. Yep, she's one lucky girl."

Chapter Eleven

The events of last night seemed blurry, disjointed. Cassie had just started a shift at the café when the sheriff called. Hurriedly explaining the situation to her boss, she had been able to leave an hour early, go home, and get packed up. After a couple of phone calls to friends and neighbors, she had her affairs arranged in order to be away for a few days. She didn't know what awaited her in Tucson, but she wanted to be at Holly's side.

The drive felt longer than ever before. Cassie had made as few stops as possible. She stayed alert fueled on coffee and adrenaline. When she arrived in Tucson, she drove straight to the hospital.

Before leaving the parking lot, she opened her trunk, and drew out a small backpack, a sweater, and a thermos filled with hot coffee. She tucked the thermos into a pocket on the side of the pack. Then she opened the flap and shoved the sweater inside. She slipped the backpack over her shoulder, shut the trunk and locked the car. Hurriedly she strode toward the hospital's main entrance.

Once she had located Holly's room, she sat at her bedside unpacking the backpack. The first thing she pulled out was Holly's NAU blanket, which she unfolded and laid over the thin cotton throw that covered Holly's legs and feet. Cassie brought the blanket up to Holly's neck, tucking it in around her.

It was a good thing she had thought to bring the warm fleece blanket. Cassie had been prepared to be cold. Hospitals always kept the temperature turned down to deter germs; nevertheless, Holly's room seemed exceptionally cold. Cassie shivered as she donned her sweater.

She reached into the pack again and brought out a pouch, which she placed on the tray table next to the bed. Inside the pouch was a collection of items including stones and herbs. This was a protective and healing spell, which Cassie had empowered before setting out on her journey to Tucson. If she had a chance, she thought she would do a little ritual, maybe some divination. She would need to be well rested for that, so it could wait.

In the meantime, she sat at the bedside while she carried on a long one sided conversation with her comatose friend. She encouraged Holly, to come back to the people who loved her. She reminded her of the future she had to look forward to, including a career in forestry, something Holly had strived long and hard for. Cassie didn't know if Holly could hear her, but she hoped that her message was getting through.

As lunchtime approached, Cassie's stomach began to rumble in protest. Reluctantly bidding Holly good-bye, she set out to find food. One of the nurses was able to direct her to a wonderful vegan/vegetarian restaurant not far from the hospital. The food was delicious, but with a full stomach Cassie found herself drowsy. *I could really use a nap.*

At that thought, she ventured back to her hotel room, lay down and nodded off. She was dreaming a disconcerting dream about Holly, the details of which were quickly forgotten when her phone rang. After the call from Dottie, she was now wide-awake, ready to shower for a return visit to the hospital.

Cassie opened her suitcase and pulled a clean outfit from the hodgepodge of clothing she had shoved into the case during her hasty packing job. She draped her clean clothes over her arm and turned toward the bathroom.

Chapter Twelve

Emeline and Holly broke their embrace when a sound startled them. Both women wiped the tears from their eyes, Holly with the back of her hand and Emeline with the delicate lace handkerchief that she had pulled from inside her left sleeve. The noise came from the mirror, a click followed by a creak. It reminded Holly of the windmill out at the Nolan's place. "Cree-aak." The mirror was opening.

Holly gasped. "Oh, my God... this could be our ticket out of here."

"Be careful," Emeline cautioned as Holly went to stand directly in front of the now open portal.

"Wow, from a mirror to a window, just like that. We can break the glass and be out of here in no time flat." Holly couldn't contain her enthusiasm.

"I do not trust that it will be that easy. Besides, what is on the other side? I think it is safer right where we are, at home."

"This is *not* home. Not anymore. We both have to leave. You need to move on to Heaven or wherever, and I have to get back to my life. I know you are afraid, but you are obviously a good person so how bad can it be? You won't find your Jonathan in here, if that's what you're waiting for."

"Yes, I understand that. You may find your way back through the mirror. Remember, I had a glimpse of your life when you were swept into the flood waters. As for me, I believe this may be my eternal home. I have no way to enter your time. My body has turned to dust."

"You have a point. I can't believe you don't have a way to contact the Spirit world. Like maybe a one-eight hundred--Heaven or at least nine-one-one. I guess you don't have cell phones or Internet on the other side."

"I have no idea what you are talking about. I wish you would not make light of my misery. Even if I do not fathom your dialect, I certainly glean much from your tone."

"I'm sorry. I get so damn frustrated that I smart off, I guess. I know you are in worse shape than I am. Hell, you've been in this room for more than a century. I can't imagine what that feels like."

"Time means nothing to me. That is a blessing. As for finding a way to leave this place, I think I might be able to call for help; I have never wanted to leave until now. I am ready to go because I know that you and Jonathan have moved on. I will never be able to join you while I remain in this place. Still, it frightens me to think of being somewhere unknown."

As the conversation continued, Holly never took her eyes off the mirror-turned-window. Nothing but shadows moved across the glass. Something or someone was out there.

At that moment, the sounds began. First scratching then rubbing, almost like fingernails on a chalkboard. Abrasive, disturbing to the ears, it continued as Holly and Emeline stared at the glass. As the noises carried on, the image on the other side became clearer. Holly thought it looked as if she were focusing a camera lens. It dawned on her that someone was cleaning the glass from the other side.

An eye came into view, a giant brown eye staring right at them. Both women jumped back, Emeline reached out to pull Holly in close beside her. Holly squirmed out of her grasp to move closer to the mirror.

"Holy shit, look at that! Who or what is it? Do you think it can see us?"

"I hope not." Emeline whispered as if the thing on the other side of the mirror could hear her.

All at once, the eye began to get smaller; the face it belonged to became visible. The "thing" was a woman. She was relaxing back in a chair. An older woman with dark graying hair, she peered into their world. The woman looked tired, sad.

"We have to let her know that we are here. What can we do?" Holly looked around for inspiration. Making a loud noise seemed like the practical choice, so her eyes spanned the room for possibilities.

"I suppose it will do me no good to caution you about placing your trust in strangers. Perhaps if we just shout she will hear us."

"There you go, stating the obvious. Let's give it a try, count to three, and then yell 'help!'"

Emeline nodded, and they moved in closer to the glass. The woman on the other side was crying, droplets winding their way down the crevices of her face. The woman began to speak, or at least she appeared to be speaking. Her lips were moving, yet the women could hear only a soft rhythmic murmuring. Startling them, the creak of the closing locket sent both Emeline and Holly into a panic.

"She closed the locket. Now what shall we do?" Emeline sidled away from the mirror. She sunk down in the rocker and began to sway back and forth.

"We wait. She will probably open it again. When I had the locket, I opened it all the time. Actually, it was like a nervous habit I had. Opening and closing it, Yeah, I did that a lot." Holly knew she was probably being overly optimistic. Still she had to hold on to the hope that the woman would want to look inside the old trinket again.

The room had become very warm. Holly, still in her shorts and tank top was sweating. She imagined that Emeline must be burning up in the heavy Victorian garb she was wearing.

"You must be ready to have a heat stroke in that outfit. I'm going to put out this fire. Not that it will help since it doesn't seem to create much warmth." Holly walked over to the fireplace. She turned to Emeline. "How should I do this? Do we have any water?"

"I will have to think about that." Emeline rested her head in her hands closing her eyes.

"What?" Holly was baffled. Sometimes she still had the feeling that she was in an institution with a crazy woman. All of a sudden, it dawned on her. Emeline had to *think* about having water in order for water to appear in the room. Just like the milk and cookies, the bed and all of the other paraphernalia that seemed to just manifest out of nowhere.

"Oh, I get it." she whispered, trying not to disturb the meditating Emeline. Quietly she made her way to the kitchen table and sat down on one of the chairs.

Within moments, Emeline pointed to a tin bucket sitting next to the door. Holly strode across the room. She looked down at the large pail. It was, as she expected, full of water. Holly lifted it with a bit of difficulty; it was quite heavy. She walked very slowly to the stone fireplace. At hearthside was a rack of tools.

Have those been there all along? Holly wasn't sure, but she was glad they were there now. In the collection was a large ladle. She used it to spoon out some of the water onto the fire to lighten the load. When the bucket was light enough, she lifted it high to pour it, dousing the rest of the flames.

Holly looked at Emeline, they both smiled. "Good job."

Emeline responded with, "Thank you, and might I say the same to you. You are very strong." They shared a chuckle.

With the fire extinguished, the room was suddenly very quiet. The women both moved to the settee, where they sat in silence. Neither knew what their next move would or should be. A familiar groan broke the stillness. The mirror was moving again. Both ladies rose, and clambered toward the glass. As the room on the other side came into focus, they saw the old woman again. She was sitting, swaying, in a hypnotic fashion.

"Now is our chance. This could be a way out of here. Are you with me?" Emeline nodded in agreement.

"Okay, one, two, three," Holly counted down. Then "HELP US!" they shouted together, as loud as they could, to the woman on the other side.

She reacted exactly as they had hoped. Her wide eyes and shocked look told them that she had heard them, and had quite likely actually seen them as well. The woman was obviously shaken. Within seconds, the cover slammed shut. Holly and Emeline stood in front of nothing but a mirror.

"Hmm, that didn't go quite as planned. At least she heard us, I'm sure of it."

"Do you think she will dare open the locket again? She might rid herself of it. If I were her, I would likely do just that."

"I think her curiosity will prevail. Even if she gets rid of it somehow, I think she will have to take another look first."

"I guess we have to wait and see. Even if she opens the locket, can she - moreover, *will* she - help us?"

"Let's just find something to take our minds off the situation shall we? Can you think us up a card game or something?"

"Perhaps. I was just remembering the nights we spent by oil lamp or candlelight. Usually we told stories until you were tucked into bed. Afterward

Jonathan and I would talk quietly while I sewed or we read until our eyes were too tired to remain open.

"Jonathan did own a pack of playing cards with which he and Mr. Eastwood played poker once or twice. I wonder where they might be."

Emeline gave Holly an amused look, and then she paraded over to the mantle above the fireplace where she stood on tiptoe feeling around behind one of the bricks. She dug out a worn cloth pouch and from it she withdrew a deck of cards. "Voila!"

After a brief discussion of card game options, they decided to play Rummy. Several rounds later, the game was all tied up. They pondered whether to play another game or not. Before they could decide they were interrupted by a voice coming from somewhere outside the room. They froze in place looking first at each other, then tentatively at the mirror.

A man's voice, vaguely familiar to Holly, was singing. Quietly, somewhat sorrowfully he crooned.

"The maid shakes her head, on her lips lays her fingers. Steps up from the stool, longs to go and yet lingers. A frightened glance turns to her drowsy grandmother. Puts one foot on the stool, spins the wheel with the other.

Merrily, cheerily, noiselessly whirring, swings the wheel, spins the wheel, while the foot's stirring. Spritely and lightly and merrily ringing, trills the sweet voice of the young maiden singing."

"That's him." Holly's heart raced. It was the man who saved her. Emotions jumbled, she looked back at Emeline, who was rising from her seat.

"Jonathan? Is that you?" she whispered.

"No, that's the voice of the man who rescued me. I remember now. He sang to me."

"He and Jonathan are the same! That man was once your father! His voice is different, but I can feel his presence and he is singing the lullaby that he always sang to you."

Holly was unconvinced. "Whoever he is, I don't think he will hear us if we don't speak up."

Holly left the table. She went to examine the mirror. The latch was still firmly in place. She wondered why they were able to hear him. They never heard anything from the other side unless someone opened the locket. *Weird*, she thought as she shook her head.

"Jonathan!" Emeline was now screaming at the mirror. The singing continued. He obviously hadn't heard her.

"Lazily, easily, swings now the wheel round. Slowly and lowly is heard now the reel's sound. Noiseless and light to the lattice above her, the maid steps, then leaps to the arms of her lover."

"He can't hear you, not unless he opens this thing," Holly declared as she jiggled the frame of the mirror. "If he is holding it, he is likely to open it, don't you think? I mean there's a good chance, right?"

Emeline was wringing her hands, biting her lip. "I hope so child, I surely do." A single tear trickled down one cheek.

Chapter Thirteen

Night had fallen, leading to a drastic drop in temperature. That was the norm in this desert town. Triple digit days gave way to nights in the seventies. As Joseph crawled into his Jeep, he relished the perfect evening. A light breeze scented with the sweet smell of acacia wafted past him.

He stood admiring the vanishing sunset. A hint of color remained in the west, red, orange and pink with a vast ocean of brilliant indigo above. A few impertinent stars, just tiny pinpoints, dotted the inky surface. Twilight was his favorite time of the day.

In the following weeks, the monsoon season would come to a close. The plants would begin to fade from various shades of green to golden umber hues. If Joseph wanted to photograph more dramatic shades, such as crimson and orange, he would drive a little over an hour away from town to Mount Lemmon, where the elevation, at over nine thousand feet afforded, a classic glimpse of fall color. His mind always seemed to wander to his love of nature and the urge to capture a bit of it on film.

Joseph was feeling on top of the world. He sang along to the radio as he drove home. The experience he had in Holly's room was unnerving, yet he still felt drawn to her. Maybe it was a good thing that he had forgotten the locket. Now he had a good excuse to visit her again. *Tomorrow, I'll take her the necklace; spend a little more time with her.*

Right now he had to focus on what he was doing. If he were to make it to the restaurant where his friends were waiting, he would have no time to waste. A shower, shave and change of clothes were in order. First, he would pop in to pick up the locket from Nonna's.

As he drove into her driveway, he noticed that no lights were on in the house. Nonna rarely left the house after dark, surely never alone. *If she went somewhere, who drove her? Sophie is at work, and Mom and Dad are still on the road. Maybe someone from church picked her up for a meeting or something.* Tentatively, he approached the door and knocked. No one answered, so he turned the knob and cautiously entered the house.

"Nonna, Nonna, are you here? Are you okay?"

"I'm in here Tesoro. Sorry, I must have turned the lights off before I sat down at the TV." Rosa's voice sounded hoarse.

Joseph found the switch on the wall in the entry, and wash of light illuminated his grandmother. She was seated in her favorite chair, in front of a dark television screen.

"Nonna, I hate to break it to you, but I think you forgot to turn on the set." He gave her a quizzical smile.

"Oh that, yes. I decided to turn it off. My mind kept wandering. Did you get my phone message?"

"Sorry, I forgot to check my phone when I left the hospital."

"You were at the hospital? I thought you were coming back here first to pick up the locket. Why did you go there without it?"

"I honestly don't know. I can't believe I didn't remember to take it to her. That's what I'm here for now, to pick it up."

"Not so fast. Since you didn't get my message, I'll have to tell you now. Sit down."

He sat on the sofa across from her. Nonna was behaving strangely, nervous and upset. Joseph thought she was about to break some bad news.

"Are you all right? Is it my mom, dad, my sisters?" Joseph mentally ran through a list of family members as his heart rate increased.

"No, no, nothing like that. I had a vision this evening."

Joseph relaxed and leaned back into the cushions on the couch. "You had me worried there for a minute. What do you mean by 'a vision'?"

"I saw something in the locket. I did a reading with the cards after I cleaned it. The reading was strange, so I tried to find out more by going into a trance like my mother used to do. You are too young to remember, but I have done it before.

"What I saw scared me. That piece of jewelry is bewitched. In a tremulous voice she breathed "Liberaci dal male, deliver us from evil."

"You should return it to the young woman and have nothing more to do with either of them." Rosa looked earnest.

"Oh Nonna, don't be melodramatic. You can't put your faith in this mumbo jumbo. You must have drifted off, had a dream. As for the card reading, you know there is nothing scientific about it. It's just a game. If you did another reading, it would probably be completely different. What exactly was frightening about that necklace?"

"I saw two women inside of the locket. They appeared to be trapped there. They called to me for help. They saw me; they looked as shocked as I was. So creepy…." Her voice trailed off as she envisioned the two faces looking out at her from behind the glass.

"Just listen to what you are saying. Obviously, you had a nightmare. It's not possible for anyone to be inside that locket. I know you are worried about me. It does seem odd that I am really attracted to Holly when I have never had a conversation with her. I guess I'm infatuated. When she wakes up, we will see if there is anything between us. Until then, don't get worked up, I can handle this, Nonna. I'm not a little boy anymore."

"I know it sounds ridiculous. Tesoro, those faces seemed so real to me. I will try to put it out of my head. I realize that you are a grown man; I apologize for hovering. There is just something very wrong about that girl and that locket."

"No need to apologize. I'll take that haunted locket off your hands now." Joseph moved over to sit on the arm of her chair; he leaned over to give Rosa a big hug. She reached for his hand, and gave it a squeeze. "All right Tesoro, follow me."

Rosa struggled up from her seat, and then led Joseph into the little hallway with the niche that housed her altar. Joseph looked over her shoulder; he saw the locket draped over the feet of the icon with three faces. He shuddered as prickles ran the length of his spine.

What if Nonna's vision really meant something? Did what she see have anything to do with the impulse he had to be with Holly or with the sudden return of the lullaby? He couldn't get the tune out of his head anytime he was near her.

He took the locket from Nonna as she reluctantly handed it over. Joseph put the necklace in his pocket.

"I have to go Nonna. Are you going to be okay?"

"Yes, I'll be fine. It's you I worry about. Are you going back to the hospital now?"

"Not tonight. I promised Ryan and some other friends that I would meet them for dinner and a few drinks at that new Sports Bar on Speedway. I'm already running late. I still have to take a quick shower."

"You better get going. Call me tomorrow."

"I will. Try to get a good night's rest. Don't fret over me."

"I'll do my best." Nonna smiled. Joseph backed out the door. He blew her a kiss and waved. As he moved his car around to his side of the lot, he called Ryan to tell him he was behind schedule. As he listened to the phone ring, he thought. *For tonight, I'm going to put this whole thing out of my mind.*

Chapter Fourteen

assie stepped out of the shower, and wrapped a towel around her dripping torso. She stood in front of the steam-covered mirror. For a second, she thought she saw Holly standing there in the mist. Beside her was a woman dressed in a long black dress, with her face veiled. Cassie blinked, and the image was gone. "I need coffee," she said to herself, wiping the mirror off with a washcloth.

Always quick to dress, Cassie soon stood before the full-length mirrored closet doors for one last look at herself. What she saw was a tall woman with a slim yet curvy figure. Her long blond hair fell down her back. The trademark bright pink lipstick she loved to wear matched the shade of her tee shirt. With the tee, she wore a pair of white shorts that set off her long tan legs. It also revealed the tattoo of a rainbow that graced her ankle. She had a gray hoodie sweatshirt tied around her shoulders in case the hospital was as cold as it had been the night before.

After she made sure she hadn't forgotten anything, she picked up her purse and backpack. She turned out the lights, walked out the door, and then wiggled the handle to make sure it had locked.

The night was clear, still. Even the sounds of traffic seemed muted. Cassie pressed the unlock button on her keychain, opened her car door and crawled in. As she pulled out of the hotel parking lot, she decided that a quick stop at Starbuck's was in order. There was one near the hospital on East Speedway.

With her favorite latte in hand, she was ready for a long night of keeping vigil at Holly's side. The doctor had discontinued the medication that sedated her friend. Now everyone was waiting for Holly to resume consciousness.

Cassie felt very optimistic as she entered the corridor outside Holly's room. The hallway was quiet as both the staff and the patients settled in for the night. At the nurse's station, a young nurse sat with her head bent over a chart. Busily writing, she didn't acknowledge Cassie as she breezed by and entered Holly's room.

Holly had been repositioned with the head of the bed more elevated than usual. Her hair had been combed so that it fell gracefully down one shoulder. She looked beautiful, peaceful.

Cassie pulled a chair next to the bed and began to unpack. She set her coffee on the bedside table and her purse on the other chair in the room. Next she removed her backpack, unzipped it and took out a variety of items including her reading materials, snacks, as well as the amulet pouch she had made for Holly, and her travel-size spell kit.

Inside a black brocade bag, Cassie's spell kit consisted of a zippered pouch containing a set of small magickal tools, some essential oils, herbs, a notebook filled with chants, spells, and notes, and packets of salt for cleansing.

Performing magickal workings or ritual in public spaces was always challenging. Most people didn't understand her religion or practices. When faced with the unknown, most humans reacted with fear. She would have to be careful.

She pushed the head of Holly's bed farther from the wall and moved her IV pole closer to the side of the bed. This made it easier to circumnavigate to create a Circle of protection around herself and Holly while she worked.

The black bag would serve as an altar cloth. She pulled the contents from the bag and laid it flat on Holly's over-the-bed table. Then she set the items on the cloth and arranged them. An athame, the ritual knife used for directing energy. A small silver chalice. Herbs, oils, salt.

She opened a small packet of salt, pouring it into the chalice, and then added a bit of water from Holly's pitcher. She dipped her fingertip into the chalice to stir. Next she began walking clockwise around Holly's bed sprinkling the saltwater, and softly murmuring "Water and salt, where you are cast, no hidden purpose or evil last, but let that only which is willed by me, as I will so mote it be." She repeated this verse three times as she continued to circle the bed.

Normally she would light candles and incense. Given the circumstances of being in a public building with fire codes, not to mention a sprinkler system, she thought it would be best to skip those elements of her ceremony.

She took up the athame and drew the shape of a pentagram in the air above Holly's head. She placed the knife back on the cloth as she picked up the spell pouch she had prepared at home. It had been consecrated for healing. It held an assortment of herbs, oils, and crystals, in addition to other objects known for their healing properties.

She reached beneath Holly's pillow and gently placed the small bag under her head. Cassie whispered in Holly's ear "God and Goddess, hear my plea, aid her in recovery. Help her heal; help her mend, strength and courage to her send. Bless her body, heart and soul. Complete recovery is the goal. So mote it be."

With her athame in her outstretched hand, Cassie retraced her footsteps around the bed, walking counterclockwise this time repeating under her breath, "This Circle is open but never broken." This she did three times. When she had finished, she gathered her belongings together and tucked them back into the brocade bag, which she put back into her backpack.

A sense of relief came over her. She had accomplished her working without interruption; now her spell could begin its magick. There was one more thing that Cassie wanted to do. She felt a strong impulse to read Holly's cards. Cassie wasn't an expert with the Tarot cards, however; she was studying with the High Priestess of her Coven, who *was* an expert. In fact, she was downright amazing. Cassie hoped to one day acquire the same knowledge and skill.

At any rate, reading for Holly would be great practice. Maybe Cassie would be able to see a good outcome for her best friend. Her cards were in her purse, so she walked over to the corner chair. She rummaged around in the bag until she located the silk pouch that held the aging deck.

She had been using this same deck since she was a young teen. It was her first tarot deck, the first of many. Despite the beauty of her other decks with their amazing artwork and imagery, she always gravitated back to this old standard set of cards with their simple design, their now worn edges.

Cassie cleared the bedside table, moving items aside as she proceeded. Inside the pouch with the deck was a tightly folded square of black fabric that she lay down on the table. She shuffled the deck, and then cut it. She placed Holly's hand over the deck, and spent a few moments in silent meditation while she allowed Holly's energy to commune with the cards. Then she began to lay down the cards upon the black cloth.

A three-card spread would do, because she wanted to make this quick. A nurse or other hospital staff could walk in any minute. It would be hard to explain what she was doing.

In the first position was the card representing Holly's past, the second her present, the third her future. Cassie lay the cards face down; one by one, she turned them over. Beginning with the past position, Cassie turned over the card.

The Tower - Inner chaos with significant life changes resulting in Holly's current situation. Cassie turned the second card, The Devil - A feeling of restriction, becoming trapped in a current situation, leading toward the future. Cassie slowly flipped the final card, Death – an end to past struggles, a door opening to new beginnings.

Staring down at the cards lined up together, she thought they looked menacing. The Tower, the Devil, Death. Even though Cassie knew that the reading wasn't necessarily bad news for Holly. She still didn't like the looks of it. A cold chill shook Cassie's body. A wave of nausea overtook her. She sat down on the bedside breathing slowly, taking deep, deliberate breaths until the feeling passed.

Gods, I feel like shit. I think I'll go back to the hotel, crash for the night. Normally, after doing a healing spell for someone, Cassie felt euphoric, energized. She would need to ground herself, either by eating, because she always had the munchies after ritual, or by sitting quietly, preferably outside, perhaps doing some breathing exercises or a short meditation.

Not tonight. Tonight she felt tired, depleted. She hoped it was just stress, not some grave omen. She gathered her gear, kissed Holly on the forehead, and then made her way to the parking lot.

Chapter Fifteen

Joseph sat next to an attractive brunette named Darcy, his "date" for the evening. They were in a booth across from his buddy Ryan and his current girlfriend, Lindsay, who was responsible for setting Joseph up with female companionship for the night. At the table next to them, Nick, Jenny and Toby were ordering another round of drinks for the group.

Joseph didn't really mind a blind date once in a while, although they never seemed to turn into anything more than a casual friendship. Tonight, however, he was distracted. He hardly heard a thing Darcy said. He felt bad about it, but he seemed powerless to shake thoughts of Holly from his mind.

"No more for me. Thanks, but I really have to head out. I'm my own designated driver." Joseph was prepared to get a lecture for leaving without offering Darcy a ride. He was usually such a gentleman; this behavior was out of character. He knew it as much as everyone else. They were now staring at him as if he had three heads.

He rose from the booth, bending down, he whispered to Darcy "I really am sorry, I'm not myself tonight. I would give you a ride, but I have someplace I have to be, and you wouldn't want to hang out there. Trust me." With that pronouncement, he waved good-bye, rushing to the door.

Ryan shrugged. "Joseph has some confusion going on in his life right now, no big deal."

Darcy smiled, lifting her fresh drink. She toasted the group to signal that she wasn't upset.

Joseph scrambled into his Jeep letting out a sigh of relief. The bar had felt oppressive. A night out with friends should have been fun. He shouldn't be thinking about Holly or taking her that damn locket. Starting the engine, he knew he had lied to Nonna and himself. He would go to the hospital and hand over the necklace. If the woman were still unconscious, he would give it to the nurse on duty. That was that.

On his way into the hospital, Joseph passed a buxom blonde with a backpack slung over one arm. She was walking quickly with a troubled look on her face. He wondered if she were there to visit a loved one.

As she rushed past, he turned his head to follow her. He caught a whiff of what he assumed was her perfume. It made him think of a commercial for herbal hair products. Once out of the hospital, she broke into a run. *That's going to be me in a few minutes. I'm going to bolt for the door too, as soon as I get rid of this.*

Joseph pulled the locket out of his pocket. *Just an old piece of costume jewelry, nothing to get worked up over.* He put it back in his pocket. *Chill out, man.* He walked with determination to Holly's room.

As he entered the room, that same herbal scent came at him again. Could that woman have been here to see Holly? He guessed it was possible; she must have regular visitors, family and friends. It was too bad that he might have missed a chance to give the locket to someone who could keep it for Holly until she recovered.

Then again, maybe she was awake now. Joseph approached the bed "Hello there beautiful. It's me, Joseph." Holly's eyes were closed. She didn't respond to his greeting. She did have more color in her cheeks than she had the last time he saw her. Her lips looked rosy and lustrous as if someone had applied lip-gloss.

Just give the locket to the nurse out there at the desk, then get the hell out of Dodge. Nope, it didn't matter what he tried to tell himself, he was going to stay for just a bit. He sat down in the chair next to the bed. He felt a little off kilter. Just one beer, that was all he'd had to drink.

Joseph was no more than a weekend social drinker, but he could hold his liquor. He shouldn't feel this loopy. He guessed that he would grab a cup of coffee, sit for a bit, sober up before going home. Between his somewhat disjointed thoughts, he realized that Holly was as restless as she had been earlier. She thrashed around on the bed, muttering under her breath. Nothing that Joseph could understand.

He left the room in search of coffee, stopping at the nurse's station to report Holly's agitation. On the way to the cafeteria, he realized that he hadn't given the locket to the nurse. In fact, the idea hadn't even crossed his mind. There was some reason he couldn't seem to turn over that item and just be done with it.

Nonna's voice rang in his ears. "That piece of jewelry is bewitched. You should return it to the young woman. Have nothing more to do with either the locket or the girl."

Coffee cup in hand, Joseph meandered down the hall to Holly's room. He still felt a little woozy as he sat back down in the chair. He sipped at the still too hot beverage before setting it down on the bedside table to cool. Holly was quieter now. Maybe the nurse had given her something. He reached over to pick up her hand. Cool and soft, he held her hand in his wondering how he could feel so strongly about a stranger.

Nonna was right about there being something spooky about all of this. If he were more metaphysically minded, he might be persuaded to listen to her warnings. Joseph was much too practical for that.

He lost track of how long he had been sitting there holding her hand. When he started to nod off, he leaned too far into the table. The rattling of the items sitting there startled him to his senses. At least he thought that at first. He looked around the room confused. Where was he? Nothing looked familiar.

He was no longer in the room, he was in a field. Tall grass surrounded him for as far as he could see. Cattle grazed in the distance. Part of the herd drank from a stock tank about a hundred yards away. He was home ... well, close to home.

He and Emeline lived just over the ridge. Tired, unsure how he came to be clear out on the edge of the property he hiked toward the Hideaway. Jonathan smiled. His mind was on a good supper and the lovely face of his bride. He took a drink from his canteen, and then began to whistle.

Joseph panicked. It was as if he were inside the head of someone else. Someone named Jonathan. He saw what Jonathan saw, felt what he felt. Crazier still, the person was whistling that lullaby, that goddamn insufferable lullaby from Joseph's childhood. The one he compulsively kept singing to Holly. Jerking himself out of the crazy dream or hallucination, Joseph jumped to his feet and fled.

Chapter Sixteen

Holly and Emeline grew weary standing in front of the mirror hoping that someone ... anyone ... would open the window to the other side. They had heard the man singing, Jonathan, or whatever name he was now using. Still, he hadn't opened the locket. Both women now sat on the chaise pondering their next move. Emeline suggested a cup of tea. She had just begun to rise from her seat, to find the kettle, when a mist began to form in the corner of the room closest to the door.

Emeline noticed it first. "What is that?" Her voice shook when she spoke. Her finger pointing, she backed away from the increasing fog-like mass that was creeping into the room. Holly turned her head following Emeline's finger.

What now? "Whoa, I don't know. Has anything like this happened before?" Holly was beginning to think that strange occurrences must be the norm in this place.

"No, I have never seen anything like it." Emeline now stood in the corner farthest from the mist.

From the cloud stepped three cloaked figures. Their white garments floated around them. In unison, they removed the hoods of their cloaks from their heads to reveal the faces of three women. It appeared that they were daughter, mother and grandmother. Their features were similar. The younger woman looked to be about the same age as Holly and Emeline.

No one spoke immediately. Finally, Holly piped up. "Who are you?"

The figures began to speak among themselves in a language that neither Holly nor Emeline could understand. As they spoke, lines of smoky vapor rose from their lips. This smoke ascended upward to the ceiling where it hung suspended.

The younger woman had fair hair that framed her lovely face; her movements were graceful like those of a ballerina. She reached into her cloak and pulled out an old-fashioned spindle with bits of silver and gold cord wrapped around it.

As Holly tried to recall the name of the middle-aged film star whom she thought the mother figure resembled, the look-alike, poised and proud, her auburn hair beautifully coiffed, pulled something from the pocket of her robe. A measuring tape.

Next, the elderly woman, her long silver hair flowing, bent down to remove a pair of sterling handled scissors from a garter just above her knee. She looked up from her slightly bent posture. Her lined face, glassy blue eyes and a mischievous smile gave her an imp-like quality.

Holly suddenly got excited. "I know you, or at least who you are supposed to be. You are the Fates, the Moirai. My roommate has a print of them; I mean you, hanging in our hallway." Holly's enthusiasm began to wane as she began to think about the significance of their presence.

The three women smiled at Holly, and continued their private conversation. Holly lowered her voice to a whisper. "Either they don't speak English or they are just plain rude."

Emeline, spellbound by the apparitions before her, stuttered, "I, I believe it is the former."

Though impossible to translate into any language spoken on Earth, the conversation between the cloaked triad progressed something like this.

"How charming. The Fates. A common ideal among the mortals." The old woman smiled and nodded at the redhead.

"Of course we do play a part similar to the role of these mythical Fates. We do intervene in the lives of human beings when they have become stuck, especially when life or death hangs in the balance."

The youngest of the three chimed in. "These two are in quite a predicament. They must certainly present a classic case."

The redhead's furrowed brow showed her genuine concern. "Emeline's existence between worlds has gone on far too long; furthermore, something has to be done about Holly. Her soul has been disconnected without the death of her physical body."

"We the Trine must step in. After we do what must be done, Holly and Emeline will be free to make choices which will ultimately determine their fates."

The old woman stepped forward and began to speak in English to Emeline and Holly.

"Many myths have been perpetuated within many cultures on the Earth in reference to us, the Trine. Many names have been bestowed upon each of us within the Trine. The Greeks called us the Moirai. They named us individually Clotho, Lachesis and Atropos.

"The Romans referred to us as the Parcae, calling us Nonna, Decima and Morta. The Norse name for our triad was the Norns, and they gave us the personal names of Uror, Veroandi and Skuld.

"We prefer to be addressed by the very first names given to us by the mortal race. We are Aya, she pointed to the young woman holding the spindle. Maya ...." She waved toward the lovely redhead. "And I am Zaya."

"Why are you here? What do you want with us?" Holly feared the answer.

Zaya was silent. The vapor that now rested beneath the ceiling began to form into long threads, three separate strands which subsequently braided themselves into a single cord. All eyes were on the activity taking place among the beams. The braided cord slowly descended, coming to rest on the shoulder of Aya who held out the spindle in front of her.

She removed the remnants of thread from the spindle and tossed them aside, leftovers from their last job. She placed the braided cord at the base of the spindle watching as it wound itself around and around until the shaft was completely covered. Aya held the spindle aloft as she walked deliberately toward the door.

Holly, exasperated by everything that had happened since she ended up in this odd prison was about to lose her cool.

Emeline moved closer to her and placed her arm around her shoulder.

"They look harmless. I think they are trying to tell us something. Calm down, and pay attention."

Holly took a deep breath. Emeline was right; she needed to adopt a wait and see attitude. She would make an effort to calm down a bit.

Once Aya reached the door, Maya moved to join her. Using her measuring tape, she began to measure out long lengths of cord, pulling the cord from both ends of the spindle to ensure that each stretch measured the same. Soon there were two piles of rope lying at her feet. She put her tape back into her pocket. She urged Holly and Emeline to come to her.

They looked at each other, uncertain whether it was best to obey this entity or not. Mentally reviewing their options, there didn't seem to be many choices. So Holly took the lead. Slipping her hand under Emeline's elbow, she led her across the room to stand in front of the two women and the two piles of rope.

Maya leaned down; she retrieved the ends of both ropes holding one in each hand. She extended her arms and offered one to Holly, the other to Emeline. She nodded to them, "Take these."

Emeline tentatively took the end of the cord in her hand. Holly looked at her as if she might disappear or turn green. She wasn't at all sure that she should trust these beings.

"Why should I take this? What's it for anyway? Is this our way out of here? I just want to get back to my life." *I'm really beginning to think this is a bad dream after all. I mean this is just too coincidental. I was just thinking about what fate had in store for us, then they show up. Cassie's print of them on the wall. I think I'm just making this whole thing up in my head. If I can control the dream, maybe I can make myself wake up.*

Maya reached for Holly's hand. She placed the rope on Holly's palm and gently closed her hand over it. Holly sighed. *I might as well go along with this.* Now that she had decided that she must be dreaming, she tried to make sense of it by assigning meaning to each image and experience. It was like solving a giant jigsaw puzzle. *Somebody wake me up from this nightmare.*

Maya placed a hand on the shoulder of each woman as she guided them both to stand directly in front of the door. The Trine backed up a few feet. Before Holly or Emeline could question, a powerful gust of wind came out of nowhere. It blew the door wide open, revealing nothing but darkness on the other side. The women glanced at each other, and at the same time, they turned toward the Trine.

Zaya, the old woman, spoke up, "Go. Follow the path. Don't let go of the rope; you will find your way. You must leave now."

As Holly grasped the rope a nervous giggle escaped her.

Emeline didn't seem amused. She looked Zaya in the eye. "Where does this path lead?"

"You will find your way to your future. Ask no more questions. Just go." Zaya's reply was a command, not a request. Both women understood that.

Zaya picked up the other end of the rope in each pile from the floor. She tied them around her waist. Emeline and Holly held hands. They held tightly to their ropes as they took a step through the open door.

The Trine waited the allotted time, and then nodded to one another in agreement; the time had come to let Emeline and Holly go. They had each chosen a path. Zaya wielded her shears, and cut through both cords. By doing so, she set the women free, and they could move on.

Chapter Seventeen

Holly and Emeline took their first tenuous step into the dark. The ground beneath their feet felt uneven. Just as they began to take small steps forward, the path suddenly lit up a few feet in front of them.

The light came from sconces set into cavernous walls on either side of them. The patchy floor beneath them resembled cobblestone. Neither woman spoke, each lost in her own thoughts.

As they walked side by side down the dim passageway, Emeline became more and more frightened. She worried about what might await her at the end of the tunnel. She should have told Holly the whole story. If she had, perhaps she would at long last have a hope of forgiveness.

She had intended to tell the truth, but when Holly actually began to sympathize with her, to feel her pain at the loss of her family ... well, at that point, it became risky to go any further. Holly might have ended up hating her.

Everything that I told Holly was accurate up to a point. Jonathan and I were indeed extremely happy together. We had made a nice home at the ranch. Then Ivy came along and Jonathan's attention was divided between us. I loved Ivy but I resented the affection that Jonathan and Ivy shared. Ivy was a bright child. She picked up on my jealousy. She was beginning to use it against me by acting out, disobeying me.

On the day that Jonathan and Ivy died, I had a trying day with the child. When Ivy defied me and left the yard to go find her father, I reached a breaking point. I stomped off to the creek in an enraged state. When I found her I began screaming at her.

By that time, the rain had picked up. The falling water felt like fuel being poured out onto the fire of my anger. Jonathan was shocked by my ranting. He stood between Ivy and me in an attempt to calm the situation.

I interpreted Jonathan's move to mean that he was defending the child, choosing Ivy over me. Something within me snapped, and I did the unthinkable. I ripped the doll from Ivy's trembling hands and tossed the doll into the rushing creek. Ivy cried out as she ran after her beloved toy.

The undercurrent immediately took her and she was swept away. Jonathan reacted as any parent should. He dove after his daughter. I lost all control. I began throwing rocks at him from the edge of the embankment. I picked up the ax, which protruded from his pack on the ground, and I hurled it in his direction.

I never expected it to connect; none of the other objects I violently pitched at him had hit their mark. Horribly, the ax struck him in the side of the head. Jonathan never knew what hit him. He collapsed into the flooding creek. I fainted.

This was not the version she had convinced herself to believe or the version she had told Holly. It wasn't the version she cared to admit to whomever or whatever awaited her on the other side. *Whatever am I to do?*

Her hands were damp. A cold sweat sent shivers throughout her being. She dropped Holly's hand, startling them both back from their ruminations. A small glimmer of light, no more than a dot, was visible way up ahead of them.

Certain that at the end of this hall, they would find freedom, they continued. The light that had been only a speck was now the size of a basketball, growing larger as they slowly advanced along the corridor. Flickering like a candle-flame it felt warm and inviting.

Emeline was beginning to feel better, safer within the tunnel, when she heard the voice. Very low, far away at first, it was the sound of someone singing. She strained to make out the melody. It was Jonathan's lullaby, yet not his voice singing it. Of course, it was him, the man Jonathan was now, in his present lifetime. *Where is it coming from? Why do I hear it now, when it seems my fate is sealed?*

"Listen, do you hear that?"

"Hear what?" Holly strained to hear. "Nope, nothing. What am I supposed to be hearing?"

"It is Jonathan, he is singing again."

"I don't hear anything. I think you are imagining things. You want to hear him, so you do. Here, take my hand again." Holly reached out, but Emeline refused.

"You think I am delusional. I know what I hear. It is Jonathan. Not his old voice, the one he has now. The voice we heard coming from the mirror." Emeline was insistent. "It is coming from over there." She pointed to her right.

"I'm sorry, I don't hear a thing. Even if he is singing, it has nothing to do with us now. We are almost out of here. Let it go."

"Alright." There was nothing else to say. Because Holly didn't hear the voice, there was no convincing her. They pressed on.

The light up ahead was now the size of a door, around it an ethereal outline of a huge portal could be seen.

Emeline wanted nothing more than to have a chance to make it right with both Jonathan and Ivy-who-was-now-Holly. It seemed as though she could not get her little family together to do that. They were living, she was not. She had caused their deaths once; she absolutely would not do that again. They would never forgive her. She would wait for them on the other side, perhaps sort out a way to make it up to them.

Hard as she tried, Emeline could not escape the singing. It was getting louder. She was positive that they were getting closer to its source. A moment of dizziness caused her to reach for the wall. She ran her fingers along the rough surface as she walked. Abruptly, the wall ended. Open space replaced it. Another tunnel branched off to the right of the main path. No lights illuminated this tributary. The song was coming from further down the black hallway.

Emeline turned to Holly, "I have to go this direction. You must realize that, at some point, we must part company. Our destinies cannot be the same. We belong to different planes of existence."

Holly looked to the spot where Emeline was pointing. She could barely see the opening in the wall. "Emeline you don't know where you are going, plus, you aren't the bravest of souls. You're liable to get lost or hurt. How about I take that path, and you stay on the main road. You aren't exactly dressed for hiking in the dark, and I'm more adventurous by nature."

"No, this is the way I should go. Jonathan is calling me to this path. You cannot even hear him."

"You mean the singing is coming from there?" Holly pointed at the dark tunnel.

"Yes, and I have to follow it. You understand that I must." It wasn't a question. Emeline wasn't going to change her mind now that it was set.

Holly looked at Emeline suspiciously "I guess, but not really. Isn't Jonathan living a new life, one that you can't join? You don't have a body anymore, remember?"

"I know. I just want to see him. I want to say good-bye." Emeline blew Holly a kiss. With that, she turned into the darkness and disappeared from Holly's view.

"Come back here now." Holly yelled in Emeline's direction. Not waiting for a response, she ran after her.

Emeline knew that Holly was in pursuit. She heard her calling out, and the footsteps behind her. She didn't see why Holly was getting so worked up about her choice. She stepped lightly as she crept down the dark tunnel, feeling her way against the wall.

The song sounded louder. Soon, she thought, she would see Jonathan, or at least his latest incarnation. Her heart leapt with anticipation. She would apologize, and then they could say their good-byes. What would happen next? She hadn't thought that far.

Emeline heard Holly's retreating footsteps as she gave up chasing after her. As the crooning voice enveloped her, Emeline began to feel strange. Her head reeled with images; thoughts became fuzzy. She was losing her memory, and she realized it.

New information crept into her mind. Old files were erased, supplanted by new ones. *Oh, my Lord, what have I done now?* She had felt this way before. Yes, it was familiar to her; it was like a birth into a new life. That is exactly what she would have thought was happening if it weren't for the fact that every memory of her life as Emeline was systematically being replaced by a memory from Holly's childhood.

Emeline tried to pull back. This was an enormous blunder on her part. There was no turning back now. A jerk of the cord and she shot forward into the darkness screaming all the way.

Chapter Eighteen

It was no use trying to catch up with Emeline in the dark tunnel. She was moving too fast, and Holly knew that short of tackling her and physically carrying Emeline back, she would not be able to get her to return to the lighted passageway.

So she turned around and walked back to the main corridor. She cautiously moved toward the now pulsing light coming from a huge partially open wooden doorway.

I hope to God that I'm wrong about Emeline. My gut tells me that I've just been duped, betrayed by a woman who claimed to have once been my mother. Maybe it was a stupid mistake, an accident. Emeline isn't that evil. She wouldn't steal my body away from me. Is that even possible? Of course, it certainly could be. Before Emeline, I didn't think reincarnation was possible. I've tried to convince myself that I'm dreaming, but I have to face the facts. This is all real and I might be as good as dead. Please let me be wrong.

The light up ahead of her throbbed in a rhythmic beat as if it were the heart of a giant being. From within the great doorway came a chatter of noise. Holly stopped to listen. *It sounds like voices.* She tried to make out the words, but she couldn't decide what the people on the other side of the light were saying.

The sounds became clearer as Holly approached the enormous gate. *Laughter, cheering, applause … it must be a party.* The joyful sounds that flowed out from the doorway were contagious. Holly felt wonderful, carefree. She was close now, almost there. *Birds, I hear birds singing.*

Holly had been holding on to the rope for so long that she had almost forgotten about it. Then, suddenly without notice, the tension on the rope broke and Holly found herself propelled forward into the brilliance ahead. As she passed through the cavernous doorway, warm rays of intense light engulfed her and an overpowering sense of peace washed over her. All memory of the past, including her time with Emeline began to fade away.

As the memories left her, she found that she couldn't let go of one tiny fragment that remained buried deep within her very being, a kernel of anger that would surface if she didn't let it go. *How can I forgive her?*

Past the threshold, she found herself surrounded by a throng of people, a welcome committee. Some were loved ones, including her parents Martin and Sandra Montgomery. Unimaginable happiness flooded over her.

Chapter Nineteen

R osa pulled at the twisted blanket, struggling to free her feet. Her tossing and turning had tangled the bedding. Now fully awake, she threw the covers back and swung her feet over the edge of the bed. Sitting up, she looked over at the clock. She had been in bed for less than two hours, yet it seemed like much longer. Gisella, Rosa's calico cat lay at the foot of the bed yawning and stretching.

"We certainly aren't getting much sleep tonight, are we kitty?"

Rosa slipped her feet into her slippers. She pulled her robe from a hook on the back of her bedroom door, tossed it over her shoulders, and then she meandered into the kitchen. Perhaps a cup of warm milk with a little honey would help her to relax. She flipped on the light illuminating the kitchen and dining area. Rosa took a cup from the cabinet, and opened the refrigerator to get the milk.

Joseph had been at the forefront of her mind since he came home from the Chiricahuas. She couldn't shake the apprehensive sensation that came over her every time she thought about his involvement with the woman, not to mention the mystifying locket. The card reading weighed heavily on her mind; the faces of the two women plagued her. Perhaps she should have done something to help them. *What could I have done?*

Joseph had said he would return the locket, and she trusted he would follow through. She wasn't as confident that he could walk away from the young lady who owned it. Rosa knew her grandson well enough to know that he was smitten.

Joseph's girlfriends fell hard for him. His response was lukewarm most of the time. He claimed to be waiting for "the one" a woman that really "got him." None of the young women he dated made him behave in the peculiar fashion that he had been exhibiting in the past twenty-four hours. The strange thing was that he hadn't had so much as a simple conversation with her.

Something was just not right; Rosa was determined to solve the puzzle. Mulling it over as she sipped at the warm milk, Rosa decided to do another reading. She rose from the table and made her way to the drawer where she kept the cards. She thought briefly about the friend who had given her this deck.

Talia was Romani, a gypsy woman who Rosa met fifteen years ago in an RV park. Joseph's parents had rented a camper trailer for a family vacation. Rosa struck up a conversation with Talia as they stood in line in the ladies room. The park was full to capacity that weekend - mostly with Talia's traveling companions, Rosa was to learn.

The two women had hit it off immediately, with Talia offering to read Rosa's cards for free. Ordinarily Talia wouldn't have socialized with a *gadzo*, someone outside the Romani culture. Nevertheless, the women spent the rest of their stay exchanging recipes, playing card games, and discussing divination techniques using the cards.

Talia called it "dukkering." Rosa smiled; she still kept in touch with Talia and thought of her every time she used this familiar old deck.

Rosa sat back down at the table removed the cards from their case and proceeded to shuffle them. She focused her mind on Joseph and the two women she had seen during her trance. Then she placed the cards face down in an abbreviated version of the last spread she used. She doubted that anything had changed drastically since her last reading, after all, it had only been a few hours ago. Two queens, three of clubs, two of spades, some of the same cards as last time and in the same positions. *What are the odds?* Even Joseph would have to believe that it was more than mere coincidence. She shook her head. Two women called to her, two kept showing up in the cards ... yet only one woman lay in the hospital, and only one had captured the heart of her Tesoro.

The clock on the wall said it was near midnight. She was tempted to call him. But he was out with his friends; it could wait until tomorrow. In the morning she would check in with him. She scooped up the cards, storing them away. She rinsed her cup, set it on the counter, and then switched off the light.

Gisella had followed her mistress into the kitchen. The cat now wove in and around Rosa's legs meowing for a treat. Rosa bent down to pick up the mewling creature. She flipped the light back on long enough to locate the pouch of kitty treats in the pantry closet. She set Giselle down to munch on the morsels. Rosa turned off the light, and padded off to bed.

Chapter Twenty

J oseph reached the hospital parking lot, having rushed out of the hospital as fast as possible without causing a stir. After all, it was nearing midnight, and he didn't want to disturb the sleeping patients. What he wanted to do was to break into a full-out run. The dream he had while sitting with Holly had him completely flustered. Joseph didn't have nightmares as a rule; neither did he recall his dreams in any detail.

This dream, however, was still crystal clear in his mind. It wasn't frightening, not really, but he wasn't himself in the dream, and that was what bothered him. No one had called him by name in the dream, yet somehow he knew that he was Jonathan.

Jonathan, I was Jonathan, I felt it, I knew it. The sensation of actually experiencing something from someone else's viewpoint really rattled him. It was in a subtle way, terrifying.

I need to talk to somebody about this. There was only one person he could think of who wouldn't laugh or freak out and call the guys in the white coats. That person was Sophia. She might give him a hard time at first; however; she would listen. She would give him some good advice.

Joseph unlocked his Jeep; he sat behind the wheel and closed the door behind him. He reached for his cell phone to check for messages. Nothing that couldn't wait, he thought. He scrolled the screen, and punched Sophia's number. As the phone rang, he wondered how he would explain the dream, and the feelings of helplessness that accompanied it. Sophia answered on the fourth ring.

It wasn't like her to answer her cell phone when she was out on a date, but she saw that it was Joseph and made an exception. Sophia turned to her date, a guy she'd met recently through friends, and smiled. "It's my cousin. I'll just be a minute." The roughly handsome thirty-something gave her a nod.

Joseph hit her with a barrage of information. "I had this nightmare earlier. It really freaked me out. I wasn't myself in the dream. I was somebody named Jonathan and it felt so real. I can't explain how weird it made me feel. Then I can't stop singing that lullaby, and I thought I saw this blond woman, once at the hospital and once in another dream. I think I'm losing it Soph."

He sounded genuinely upset, so Sophia tabled her usual jesting tone. "Calm down, you're going to be fine." She hoped she was right.

"Sorry Soph, I think I must be overtired. I just realized you are at work. Crap. Wait, you don't usually answer your phone at work."

"Actually, believe it or not, I'm on a date." She laughed, as she watched the man next to her. He was shaking his head and making 'hang-up' signals.

"Ah, jeez. I'll let you go. But I'm confused, why aren't you at work?"

"I was sent home early because they are short-handed for tomorrow morning and need me to go back in then."

"Burning the candle at both ends eh?"

"Something like that. It's okay that you called. Here's what I think. I think you are experiencing a mild case of PTSD. It isn't that unusual for people who undergo a frightening event; like your rescue of Ms. Montgomery from a flash flood, to undergo a measure of post-traumatic stress. You will probably get over it soon enough, especially after she wakes up and hails you as her hero."

Joseph could feel the encouragement in her voice. She was right; that made perfect sense. *Why didn't I think of that?* He was glad that he had called. Sophie's no nonsense demeanor was just what he needed.

"Thanks, cuz. I'm sorry I called during your date. Have fun."

"No problem, Joseph. Go home, get some sleep."

"Later." Joseph set the phone down in the console before starting the Jeep. Sleep was not going to come easy; he feared it was going to be a long night. For the time being, as he pulled out of the parking lot into traffic, the only thing he wanted to focus on was getting home safely in spite of the crazy drivers on a busy weekend night.

Minutes later the Jeep eased into the driveway of Joseph's casita. As he climbed out of the truck, he noticed that Nonna's house was dark, and the neighborhood was silent, except for the house on the corner where a party was in full swing. Guests called to each other, car doors slammed. Music blared from the speakers that sat just inside the garage, the door of which was open.

The interior was ablaze with lanterns. Laughter spilled from the open doors and windows of the house. It appeared to be a celebration of some sort, maybe a birthday. Whatever the reason for the gathering, Joseph hoped that it would wind down soon. If he were to get any rest tonight, he would need some peace and quiet.

Joseph left the Jeep, strode to the front door, and turned his key in the lock. He turned on a lamp and made his way into the kitchen, where he switched on the overhead light. Next he readied the coffee maker for the morning.

Afterward, Joseph proceeded to the bathroom. He threw off his clothing, and turned on the shower. He may have had a quick rinse off earlier in the evening but his experience in Holly's room had left him feeling hot, sweaty and fatigued. He stood under the soothing hot water and felt his tense muscles relax under the steaming stream. He took his time shampooing his hair and soaping his body. Clean and refreshed, he stepped out and toweled off. Then Joseph wrapped the towel around his waist before he pulled a comb through his hair.

He left the balmy bathroom behind him, and went to his bedroom dresser where he took out a pair of boxer shorts. He tossed the towel into a hamper near the dresser, and then pulled on the shorts. Wearily he flopped down on the bed. *Oh yeah, the necklace.*

Rolling off the bed, he strode over to the pile of discarded clothing and pulled the locket from his jeans pocket. With the locket in his right hand, he picked up the heap of clothes with his left and threw them into the hamper with the towel. "Two points!"

Clutching the locket, he went back to the bed, pulled the covers back and crawled in. He laid there for a few minutes, his thoughts drifting from one thing to the next. Before long, he was asleep with the locket still firmly clasped in his hand.

Chapter Twenty-One

Sunday morning dawned in pale pinks and bittersweet corals that matched the array of fresh fruits on Cassie's breakfast plate. She sat on the small deck of her hotel lobby watching the sunrise, enjoying the free continental breakfast offerings. She chose vanilla yogurt, grapefruit slices, a tangerine and a banana. A cup of coffee with a touch of cream sat next to her plate.

Cassie had a good feeling about the day, and it showed in her unusually sunny disposition. She was not ordinarily a morning person. Now she was up at dawn, dressed in a floral sundress and sandals, having an early meal. This was the day that Holly would regain consciousness. She just sensed it. Centering her psyche on the power of positive thinking she finished her breakfast, then set off for the hospital.

The nurses from the night shift were completing their paperwork. They had just finished updating the day shift on patient care and conditions when Cassie arrived at Holly's floor. She stopped at the nurse's station, to inquire about Holly's night. The nurse told her about Holly's restlessness. She also mentioned that a young man had visited Holly.

The nurse told Cassie that the man had left in haste. In fact, she had said that he "lit out of here like his pants were on fire." Cassie's curiosity was peaked, she wondered to herself if it was the guy who rescued Holly from the flood. If it was, she hoped he would be back so she could thank him.

Holly had been positioned on her side with two pillows propping her up. Her room again felt extremely cold to Cassie when she entered. The light sweater she was wearing over her sundress did nothing to keep her from shivering; her bare legs were covered in goose bumps.

Holly is going to freeze. She tucked Holly's covers in tightly around her. Then Cassie threw the extra blanket she had brought from home over her own shoulders and huddled under it as she sat down in the chair next to Holly's bed. She must have dozed off because the next thing she knew she was startled awake by a scream.

When Holly woke, it was as if she were surfacing for air after a near drowning. She gasped, and a blood-curdling scream escaped her lips. Her eyes flew open as she fearfully struggled to sit up. *Where am I, who am I?*

She panned the room, her mind a blank canvas. Within seconds, pieces of a puzzle began to collate in her brain. She recognized the trappings of a hospital room, and that triggered memories of the accident. Holly then remembered her name and details of her life made their way to the surface of her conscious mind. As her foggy mind slowly cleared, she found that she had no concept of time.

I wonder how long I've been here, out of it. What have I missed while I've been asleep? I had a terrifying nightmare, but I can't remember anything about it

When Holly screamed Cassie almost fell off of the chair. She rushed to Holly's side, resting an arm around her. Holly was shaking, staring straight ahead, her eyes darting about the room. She seemed unaware of Cassie's presence. Cassie pressed the call button clipped to the side of Holly's bed and waited for a nurse to arrive. As the sudden shock wore off, Cassie murmured. "Holly, it's me, Cassie. Do you recognize me?"

Holly wasn't so certain. The face was familiar, so was the voice. "Uh, yes, I think so."

"Good, great. I mean, damn girl, you had me worried. Do you feel alright? Any pain?"

"I feel tolerable well. My head aches a bit, not too much." *Tolerable well, that sounds weird, why did I say that?* Holly lifted her hands up to her head; she felt for bandages and then lowered them back to her lap, relieved to find that she hadn't apparently suffered a grave head injury. *I feel really confused.*

"Well, I for one am thrilled to have you back among the conscious. Do you remember your accident?"

The accident, yes, it's coming back to me. "I think so. I was up on the mountain and it was raining. I remember my truck got stalled out in the wash and then I saw a wall of water. That's the last thing I remember, except for the singing."

"The singing, do you mean ringing? Your ears were ringing?"

"No, I heard a man singing to me. He had a soothing voice. Cassie, how long have I been here? How did I get here?"

"You've only been here a couple of days, just since Friday night, and today is Sunday. You didn't miss much.

"You were rescued by some guy that just happened to be coming off the mountain at the right time to see your truck go floating by. He pulled you out of the creek. You can thank him and that crazy yellow jacket of yours. I guess the fabric of your jacket got stuck on a mesquite bush and kept your head out of the water. You are one lucky lady." Cassie grinned.

Holly watched Cassie with interest as she explained the details surrounding her accident. She knew that Cassie was her best friend, at the same time she seemed like a complete stranger.

The next few hours were a flurry of activity. The nurse assessed Holly's physical condition and determined that her vitals were all normal, and then she called the doctor. He just happened to be in the hospital at the time; therefore, he was able to take a look at Holly and talk with her right away. The wheels were set in motion for Holly to receive follow up care as well as a psychiatric evaluation, given that she was a trauma victim.

During this whirlwind of response to Holly's awakening, Cassie mothered over her and made sure that she was comfortable. She also talked almost non-stop as she nervously tried to catch Holly up on everything. Holly nodded her head a lot doing her best to follow along with the conversation.

"I brought you some clothes to wear home. Just shorts and a tee-shirt, that okay?"

"Uh, sure, I guess so." Cassie's words made little sense. *Underclothing, it seems she has brought me only undergarments. What is a tee shirt?*

"I think the guy who saved you might have been here to visit you last night. One of the nurses said that a young man was here. I must have just missed him."

"Yes, I think he was here." The notion that the man had been there excited her. *It was him, the man who sang to me. I'm sure of it. What a peculiar thing for him to do, considering that we are not even acquainted.*

Holly felt as though she had been gone a long time. Her summer in the mountains, school, the events leading up to the accident ... they all seemed to be a distant memory, a hazy one at that.

Chapter Twenty-Two

Joseph woke up later than he had planned. It felt good to sleep in, even if it meant that he missed getting some early morning shots of the birds congregating at the numerous bird feeders on the patio. He must have needed the extra sleep, because he had been out cold.

When he woke, he was pretty much in the same position as he had been when he fell asleep. The locket was still wrapped around his hand. He unwound the chain from his hand, noting the marks it left on his skin. He set the locket on his nightstand.

Stretching, Joseph yawned as he walked to the bathroom. He emerged freshly shaved and ready for the day. He dressed in a pair of khaki cargo shorts with a navy striped tee shirt. He loaded his pockets with wallet, keys, and lastly, the locket.

He stood in front of the refrigerator bemoaning the fact that he had put off going to the grocery store as long as possible. With nothing left to make a decent breakfast, Joseph resolved to make a trip first to the coffee shop; then he would stop at the Fry's grocery on the corner for a few staples. As he set foot outside, he breathed in the aroma of a honeysuckle vine that trailed over the lattice on the side of the house. He inhaled deeply as he enjoyed the sweet scent.

It made him hungry. He daydreamed of donuts as he locked the house and unlocked the Jeep. Once again, he noticed that he had left his phone in the car. It was a bad habit that he needed to break. *I have to get used to putting it in my pocket, or I'll have to buy a case for it that clips to my belt.* He picked up the phone and plugged it into the car charger. He looked to see if anyone had called.

Sophie's message was vague, but intriguing. He didn't want to jump to conclusions because Sophie tended to exaggerate. Her phone had rung only twice before she answered. "She's awake."

Just two words, but they sent Joseph reeling. He hit Sophie with a battery of questions that she didn't have the answers to. "That's all I know Joseph. Mona, one of the nurses, told me that she is awake and seems alert. If you want to know more, you will have to come down here and find out for yourself. I, unfortunately, have a job to do."

"Sure, I understand. I'm on my way now. Thanks."

"Of course. I know how anxious you've been. Now maybe you can go back to being your old self. I'll talk to you later."

Joseph pulled into the drive-through, where he ordered coffee and a bagel. From there he turned toward the hospital. He decided to forgo the grocery shopping; it could wait. The closer he came to Holly, the more nervous he felt. His stomach was churning, much like it did the morning after he ate takeout tacos. His heart felt as if it might beat its way out of his chest. *Get a grip.* He gave himself a pep talk as he navigated traffic, which wasn't bad on a Sunday morning.

The Jeep was too big to fit in the only parking slot available in the lot. Joseph had to navigate the parking garage. Once parked, he couldn't think of what he had done with the locket. Searching his pockets, he was relieved to find it there. He took it out and looked it over. Finally, he would be able to return it, get back to life as usual.

He stopped a nurse in the hallway to ask if Holly felt fit enough for some company. "I'll find out." She wandered down to Holly's room and peered around the corner. Joseph stood back, waiting.

"Ms. Montgomery has another visitor. Should I send him in?" The nurse directed her question to Cassie.

"Holly, this might be the guy." Cassie looked at Holly with a question on her face. "Are you ready to meet him?"

"Yes. Send him in."

Chapter Twenty-Three

The nurse turned back to Joseph, giving him the okay sign. He moved into the doorway. Holly sat up and straightened her gown. She wished she had been given enough warning to have a look in the mirror, to run a brush through her hair. She sighed, knowing she didn't look her best.

The man at the door was drop dead gorgeous, at least by Holly's standards. She loved his dark curls and deep-set eyes. *Just my luck, that I would meet someone like him on these terms.* Of course, he had seen her before, probably looking worse than she did now. She envisioned a drowned rat.

Joseph approached the women. "Hi, I'm Joseph, Joseph Romano. I am the guy that stumbled onto the accident, out at Turkey Creek." He extended his hand.

Cassie rose and took his hand. "Pleased to meet you, Mr. Romano. Or do you prefer Joseph?"

"Please, call me Joseph." Joseph recognized Cassie as the woman with the herbal fragrance that he saw rushing from the hospital the night before.

"I'm Cassie Reagan - and this is my best friend, Holly Montgomery. I guess you two have already met, sort of." Cassie turned to wink at Holly. "I want to thank you for saving my b-f-f. I don't know what I would do without her."

"I was just in the right place at the right time, I guess." As Joseph talked with Cassie, his eyes wandered to Holly who restlessly watched. *My palms are sweaty. Ugh.* She discreetly wiped them off on her blanket.

Cassie stepped aside "I'm going to let you two get acquainted. I'll be downstairs in the cafeteria getting snacks."

Joseph moved closer to Holly "How are you feeling?"

"Pretty good. I want to thank you myself. I guess I owe you my life. 'Thank you' doesn't seem like enough." Holly smiled as she looked him in the eye.

Joseph sat in the chair next to the bed. Their initial nervousness at meeting melted quite quickly, and soon Holly was asking Joseph to track down a mirror so that she could assess the damage.

"You look beautiful to me." She did. Her hair, though not perfectly smooth, gave her a tousled sexy look.

Holly found that the handsome young man was quite down to earth. She felt at ease with him, comfortable. He carried himself with an air of confidence, yet he wasn't at all cocky or full of himself. There was an intimacy between them that denied the newness of their acquaintance. Holly felt it. *I could swear that we've known each other for ages.*

Joseph pulled the necklace from his pocket. "I found this at the creek. It was lying beneath you after I pulled you out." He handed her the locket.

Holly took it from him reluctantly. "Yes, it's mine. I found it up at the Hideaway, the ranch I was just telling you about." They had discussed her summer job, as well as her plans to finish school next semester.

"You don't look too pleased to have it back." Joseph's face showed his disappointment. It would have been ironic if she didn't care about the old thing after all of the drama it had caused him.

"I don't know. Something about it makes me uneasy. It's probably because of the sad story connected to it." As she told Joseph what she knew, about the widow who had lost both her husband and her daughter, it occurred to her that somehow she knew more of the tale now than she had before her accident. *That is strange. Is it feasible that I dreamt about the ranch and the locket while I was in my medically induced coma?* "Thanks for keeping it for me."

As they talked, Holly thought about the song that she was sure she had heard Joseph sing. She asked him about it.

"You didn't sing a song to me did you?" She was pretty sure he had. It was his voice she remembered.

"Actually, I'm guilty. It's an old lullaby I know from when I was a kid. It just came back to me out of the blue." He left out the disturbing fact that when he was around her the tune haunted him. Joseph also failed to tell her about his nonna's card reading and the illusions he was experiencing.

"Will you sing it for me again?" Holly begged with her eyes.

When Cassie returned, she found Joseph sitting on the side of the bed, holding Holly's hand, singing to her. Cassie's expression must have belied her amusement. Before they could explain, Holly's doctor entered the room accompanied by two nurses. He needed to examine Holly, so Cassie and Joseph took the cue. They left the room, but promised to return later in the day.

Chapter Twenty-Four

H olly was sent home. Cassie vowed to watch over her. Her physical recovery was steady, even if she resisted the trips to therapy, both physical and mental. Both women were relieved when all of the doctors signed off on her case and they didn't have to make any more trips to Tucson for treatment.

Joseph and Holly took turns visiting each other as they continued the friendship that began after Holly regained consciousness. After Holly graduated at midterm, the relationship deepened. They spent a lot of their free time calling, texting, and emailing each other. Joseph laughed at Holly's 'hunt and peck' texting skills.

Weekend visits became a regular thing. Joseph made the trip to Flagstaff most of the time because it took Holly awhile to get the hang of driving again. It was as if she had never been behind the wheel.

Holly's frustration was evident when she tried and failed to do things that had been second nature to her before the accident. One such instance occurred on a day when Cassie was at work and Holly wanted to surprise her by cleaning the apartment before she got home.

Holly warily approached the wall outlet. She held the plug on the end of the vacuum cleaner cord in a death grip. *This is ridiculous; I know that I'm not going to be electrocuted by the thing.* She plugged the machine into the receptacle, and then hastily retreated to the other side of the living room. The Hoover sat innocently waiting for her.

She pulled a pair of earplugs from her pocket and inserted them into her ears, and then she flipped the switch on the machine and gritted her teeth at the alarming whir. *It has to be done; I guess there is no time like the present.* She pushed the vacuum around the rooms of the apartment with a vengeance.

The doctors had told her that everything looked normal. She had been too afraid to tell them how disconnected she sometimes felt. If the experts weren't worried, then she wouldn't worry either. Still the random thoughts that made no sense and her forgetfulness troubled her.

I don't know why I can't remember how to operate electronic devices, computers, even my cell phone. It happens all the time. Holly thought she was pretty good at covering the lapses in her memory, although she suspected that Cassie was aware of the problem.

One fix that she had discovered was that if she walked away from the equipment and came back a few minutes later her knowledge and abilities would be restored. *My mind must have a reset button.*

There were other things too, like the changes she had felt compelled to make to her appearance. Her clothing, hair, and make-up were all different now. Maybe that was just a normal change in style preference, though she didn't think so. Something was not right, but she wouldn't let it ruin her life with Joseph. He hadn't known her before the accident, so he was none the wiser.

Holly's worst fear was that the people closest to her would think something was wrong with her. She felt fine and didn't want any tests or, Heaven forbid, counseling. She had had quite enough of head shrinkers after her parents died. She just needed a little more time. She would be fine.

Chapter Twenty-Five

It had been a year since Holly's accident, and Cassie was at her wits' end. Ever since Holly returned home to their apartment, it had been an uphill battle. For Holly, everything was a struggle. Finishing out her doctor's appointments for follow up, getting to class, even socializing with friends seemed overwhelming. One thing that Holly could manage to do without constant prodding was to keep in touch with Joseph.

Cassie didn't understand it. Before the accident, Holly was independent, headstrong and sure of herself. She had been dead set against any man changing that. Now, according to Holly it was true love that had transformed her. Joseph was now her number one priority.

Cassie sat in the austere office waiting for Holly's doctor to arrive. She went through the catalog of concerns that monopolized her thoughts. Dr. Muleta had agreed to see her somewhat reluctantly. The doctor, communicating through his nurse, told Cassie that he would not be sharing any medical information. Cassie hoped that he could answer her questions within his self-imposed constraints.

Outside the wind blew through the parking lot, strewing leaves and sand about before whipping into a small dust devil. It blew the ball cap off a young man's head as he walked to his car, forcing him to jog after it. He caught up to it when it landed in a hedgerow bordering the lot. Cassie watched as she fidgeted in the uncomfortable chair.

The small office was painted a dull green with a slate-colored tile floor. Cassie sat in one of two straight-backed chairs upholstered in black vinyl. The doctor's large swivel chair sat on the other side of a massive oak desk that dominated the room. The top of the desk was bare aside from a photo, in a black frame, depicting the doctor with a young woman holding a trophy. She was probably his daughter. On the wall behind the desk were framed copies of the doctor's degrees, along with news clippings of various articles featuring his prowess as a neurologist. He was proficient in his field, of that there was no doubt.

Driving down to Tucson and making this appointment had been a last ditch effort on Cassie's part to understand what was happening to her old friend. She crossed and uncrossed her legs; she rubbed her cold hands together as she anxiously waited. After what seemed like an hour, but was really half that, the doctor entered the office, closing the door behind him. He offered Cassie his right hand; in his left, he carried a small computer case.

She rose to greet him and they shook hands. He was taller than Cassie remembered, though she had only seen him briefly once before. His eye-glasses were perched on top of his dark but graying hair. A white lab coat covered most of his clothing, and a stethoscope dangled from one of the coat's side pockets.

When they both were seated, Cassie began to tell him about the changes in Holly since her accident. "She doesn't want to participate in the things she always enjoyed, like mountain biking. Also, she has her guard up all the time, like she's hiding something. Believe me, Holly's personality has changed, Doctor. Now she is such a prude, she gets flustered if she accidently drops the f-bomb. Then, of course, she's obsessed with Joseph, the guy who rescued her."

Dr. Muleta sat quietly listening. His facial expression was unchanging, giving Cassie no clue as to what he was thinking as she rambled on. When she had spilled her avalanche of concerns before him, she took a breath and waited for a response.

The doctor leaned forward on his desk. He pulled a pen from the front pocket of his coat and twirled it between his fingers for a few seconds, collecting his thoughts.

The woman before him was a sight to behold. Stunningly beautiful, but rough around the edges. She had evidently tried to dress conservatively. Her hair was pulled up and fastened with a silver clip; she wore a tweed skirt, blouse and pumps. Yet there were telling signs of a much more liberal Cassie. It was evident in her speech and mannerisms, but the gay pride key chain on her handbag was what interested the eye of Dr. Muleta.

Before agreeing to speak with Cassie, he had gone over Holly's file carefully. "There is nothing here in her records to cause concern." He held up his Netbook. "Medically, she is in good health. Her scans and all of her blood work are normal. The psychologist who followed up with her after the accident has signed off on her case. No problems were noted. These facts in mind, I feel sure that whatever worries you have may be unrelated to Holly's accident."

"Are you sure, Doctor? All of these changes in her behavior started after the accident."

"Yes, Miss Reagan, I'm sure. I think I understand the problem."

"What is it, then, if it isn't physical or psychological?"

"I think it's a case of jealousy. This Joseph has come between you. Perhaps you have feelings for Holly that you haven't acknowledged in the past. I can recommend a therapist...."

Cassie was outraged, yet she tried to maintain her composure. "Holly and I have been best friends since junior high. Just because I happen to be a lesbian does not mean that I am in love with every female I have a relationship with. Holly is my friend, not my lover."

"Now calm down Miss Reagan. I was only posing a possibility."

"She just isn't the same. She's more timid, quieter. It's like the old Holly has been replaced."

"Listen to yourself, Miss Reagan. Correct me if I'm wrong: you are upset that Miss Montgomery no longer swears? You are angry that your friend has matured? She isn't the college girl she was. She has a career and a loving relationship. Both of which make her happy. You said that yourself. Are you sure that envy isn't motivating your concern?"

Cassie was livid. It was all she could do not to fly into a rage, to cause a scene. Somehow she managed to pull herself together enough to politely say good-bye to the doctor and his nurse on the way out.

Once she was in her car, she burst into tears. She sat there for a while, pondering Dr. Muleta's words. Maybe there was a grain of truth to them. Not that she had romantic feelings for Holly, but that she did envy - a little bit - the relationship she had with Joseph. She wanted that kind of love for herself one day.

It would be hard to lose Holly if she and Joseph decided to get married. They might even move out of state. Cassie decided she better enjoy her friend's company while she had it. She could ignore the changes in Holly's personality. After all, for the most part Holly was the same person she had always been.

Chapter Twenty-Six

R osa took the pies from the oven. They smelled delightful. Ricotta pies were an old family favorite, the sweet crust with a hint of chocolate and lemon in the filling. She had made them especially for Joseph because he loved them so much.

It was a rare treat these days that he was to come for a visit this morning. Between the new job that he had taken with an online travel agency, taking photos for their ever-expanding catalog, and his whirlwind courtship of Holly, Joseph seldom visited for more than a few minutes. Today he had asked to spend the day.

Joseph tapped at the door, announcing himself as he entered Rosa's house. The aroma of the pies overtook him. "Oh Nonna, those pies smell incredible. Are they cool enough to cut?" He was practically drooling as he headed to the kitchen.

"Give them a few minutes, Tesoro. I just took them out of the oven. Have a seat." She motioned to a chair at the dining table.

Joseph sat down. "Have any coffee made?"

"I was just going to ask you if you wanted coffee or if you would prefer some tea. I have that herbal tea you like."

"Coffee would be great. I think I need the caffeine." Joseph sighed and yawned.

"Late night?" Rosa inquired as she poured Joseph's coffee along with a cup for herself, placing them on a tray with a creamer from the fridge, a sugar bowl, and two spoons.

"Yep, Holly and I saw the midnight showing of a new movie that she was dying to see."

"You've been spending a lot of time with her haven't you?" Rosa walked to the table and set the coffee tray down.

"Yes, I have. That's kind of what I wanted to talk to you about today."

"I thought so. You have never been so taken with a girl before." Rosa didn't want to rehash all of her apprehensions regarding Holly, the locket, and the card readings. Her first meeting of the girl had been disconcerting.

Rosa thought Holly looked very similar to one of the women in her vision, yet she knew that she was probably just imagining it. In reality, the young woman was very nice and polite; Rosa had no good reason not to like her.

"I know you have your reservations, but Nonna, I really love her. In fact, I plan to ask her to be my wife." Joseph waited for a reaction.

"You're going to propose? Aren't you rushing this? What has it been, a year? You don't even see each other that often." Rosa knew her words were falling on deaf ears.

"Now that Holly has graduated we see each other much more often. I know you don't approve. I really want your blessing. If you just try to get to know her better, I know you will love her."

"What do your parents say? Do they love her?" Rosa sat down across from Joseph; she put her hand on his arm.

"They are happy for me, Nonna. Yes, I think they really do love her." Joseph looked his grandmother in the eye.

"Alright then, I guess I am outnumbered. You have my blessing. I am happy for you." Deep down she wanted to scream. Something was very wrong with Holly. Rosa knew it.

But if she said anything, everyone would think that she was just a jealous grandmother, resentful of any woman who would take her beloved grandson away from her. Rosa would have to play along.

"Let's have some of that pie to celebrate. Now I just have to hope that she says 'yes'." Joseph grinned.

Rosa got up to retrieve the pie. She walked into the kitchen and pulled the oven mitts from the drawer where she had placed them earlier after removing the two pies from the oven. She picked up one of the still very warm pies and gingerly carried it over to the table. Placing it on a ceramic trivet, she went back to the kitchen for plates and forks.

The two sat and talked, enjoying the pie and each other's company. Nothing more was said about Joseph's plans with Holly.

Chapter Twenty-Seven

"The garden will be beautiful this time of year. Joseph's grandmother will be bringing in some extra flowers for color. She is borrowing potted plants from a friend who is a member of Desert Gardeners. She reportedly has the best garden in town.

"Of course, Rosa's garden is pretty without the extras. The Palo Verde trees surround the courtyard, and there is a cactus garden in one corner. Some plants are still blooming, including the trumpeting sacred datura, scarlet sage, and violet verbena, as well as the silver-leaf nightshade." Holly was as giddy as a child at Christmas-time.

Cassie listened with feigned interest. It was still a shocker that the wedding was only a few days away. Joseph had proposed in August, just two short months ago. *Why the rush?* Cassie had wondered.

The thought that Holly might be pregnant crossed her mind. She had actually asked Holly outright if that were the case. Holly adamantly denied it. For that matter, she seemed offended by the suggestion. Lately, the mere mention of sex embarrassed Holly, as if she were a demure Victorian damsel.

That was another quirk that came about after the accident. Holly hadn't been a virgin since high school. Even though she certainly didn't play it fast and loose, she shouldn't act as if she and Cassie hadn't discussed their sex lives on occasion.

"Are you listening to me?" Holly snapped her fingers at Cassie in frustration. "It feels useless to discuss the wedding details with you, Cassie. I wish that you were excited for me. You act like you don't like Joseph or something."

"Of course I like Joseph, it just seems like you are jumping into this in a hurry."

"We've been dating for a year. There is something else bothering you, isn't there?"

Cassie shook her head. "No, nothing. I'm listening. Are you sure the weather will hold out for a garden wedding?"

"We checked the forecast; it looks as though it will be nice. Just in case we have a Plan B. Rosa is going to let us clear the Arizona room in the back to use if it gets cold."

"I thought Joseph's grandmother was lukewarm over your engagement. Did she change her mind?"

"Not really. She still looks at me like I'm going to devour Joseph in one bite. For his sake, she is trying; she has been very sweet to let us use her court-yard, and now part of the house, for the wedding and reception. Hopefully she will warm up to me."

"Maybe it's your choice of friends that bugs her. She keeps a pretty close eye on me when I've been around her. I don't think she has a very high opinion of me, either, if it makes you feel any better." Cassie chuckled when she visual-ized Rosa's disapproving gaze.

The evening before the big event, Cassie's parents hosted a dinner at a local restaurant. Rosa offered to cook for everyone and host the dinner at her house. However, after much discussion, all parties agreed that cooking the dinner and catering the wedding was too much for Rosa to take on. So, the group met at the much-acclaimed venue.

Cassie had tried, on several occasions, to have a serious conversation with Joseph regarding the many changes that took place in Holly after her mishap. She was afraid that he didn't really know the woman he was mar-rying. If Holly began to behave like her old self, perhaps Joseph would not be happy. Cassie had to at least voice, her concern before they tied the knot. *Tonight is my last chance. I have to get him alone long enough to talk about my fears.*

Later, between courses, she found her opportunity. Cassie's mother asked Holly to follow her into an adjoining room, where she planned to give her a beautiful lace garter for her 'something borrowed'. While they were away from the table, Cassie moved to sit in Holly's vacant chair next to Joseph. "I really need to talk to you", she said in a hushed tone.

Joseph rose from the table, and excused himself. He headed toward the hallway at the back of the restaurant where the restrooms were located. Cassie followed a few minutes later "I think I'll make a trip back there myself."

Joseph stood in the foyer at the end of the hall. "So what's up? You have a secret wedding surprise?" He was grinning from ear to ear.

"Well, no …. I mean, it's no surprise. Frankly, I'm worried about Holly. You know I'm always giving her weird looks, asking her questions about her behavior."

"Yes, I know you think she hit her head too hard in the accident. Holly has shared with me some of your concerns. It doesn't seem like a real Jekyll-and-Hyde thing. She is just more cautious, which is understandable, don't you think?"

"I'm not sure you understand the changes in her personality. What if she stops doing the little behaviors that you think are charming? If she starts to act like her old self, will you still feel the same way about her?"

"I appreciate how much you care for Holly, I really do. But there is nothing that could make me love her any less. If anything, she might come to her senses and dump me someday." Joseph smiled at Cassie laying his hand on her shoulder. "You're a good friend."

"Just so long as you know that you are marrying the pod-person Holly, not the real one." Cassie quipped.

"Of course, a sci-fi reference. Let me guess. *Invasion of the Body Snatchers*, right?"

"Your inner nerd is showing." Cassie laughed. "But do you know the book or the movies? Did you know that there are four films? The first was made in 1956, a year after the book was written. The last was made in 2007. In it the pod people became a virus."

"No, I did not know all of that. You win the dork award." Joseph sighed and rolled his eyes.

"It's geek, not dork. Need I explain the difference?"

"No, I think I'll survive without that knowledge. You can rest assured that I love my little pod person. Even if she mutates, I will be there for her. Thanks for taking such good care of her."

"Okay, I feel better now. But that's just it. You say that I'm taking care of her. It was always a two-way street before the bump on the head. We looked out for each other. I can't tell you how many times she defended me against bullies and mean spirited people. It wasn't easy growing up different. Being Pagan on top of being gay was a double whammy. I guess I'm just not used to always playing the protector."

Cassie leaned against the wall. She was relieved to talk to someone about this, finally. Joseph had turned out to be a good friend. She thought Holly would be fine with him at her side.

"How's this, I'll look out for you both, and you can return the favor - how about that?" Joseph put his hand out; Cassie took it giving it a squeeze.

"It's a deal." Cassie retreated into the ladies' room. Joseph headed back to the table, where Holly waited for him.

Chapter Twenty-Eight

The day of the wedding was warm and still. A clear blue sunny sky with only a few wispy clouds overhead made for a perfect day. The garden courtyard of Rosa Romero's little house was decked out in fall color.

In addition to the flowers in bloom and the potted annuals borrowed from her friend, baskets of Indian corn, squash, and pumpkins adorned the low block wall, which ran along one side of the patio. Chairs had been set up facing an arbor adorned with tiny lights. Pretty silk ribbon in crimson and copper hues had been tied in amongst the various flower arrangements, adding to the festive autumn theme.

The back covered porch, just off the Arizona room, had been transformed into a banquet area with tables set up for food and cake. A smaller table sat to one side for gifts. Lanterns hung from the beams above the porch, and torches lined the perimeter of the courtyard to provide lighting for the evening ceremony and celebration.

Cassie's friends from a band calling themselves Rowan Tree agreed to play for a reduced fee. Everything was coming together nicely. Rosa, in spite of her reservations, looked pleased as she sat on the patio assessing the scene. She wanted Joseph to get married in the church, and she had encouraged him to talk to the priest, but Joseph had his own ideas. After discussing it with Holly, they agreed that a less formal ceremony was more their style.

The ceremony would be everything Joseph and Holly had hoped for. Holly looked beautiful in the vintage gown she bought in a tiny retro shop on Fourth Avenue.

The color of the feminine lace was called shell, a pink-beige that was per-fect next to her summer-tanned skin. It had three-quarter length bell sleeves and a two-tier bottom. The front top edge came to a point and was trimmed in satin. A beautiful lace rose of the same lace material as the dress graced the plunging neckline.

Holly stood in front of the mirror in Rosa's small bathroom. She adjusted her clothing and applied her make-up. Everything was perfect. Joseph would soon be her husband. Now if only her parents could be there. She tried not to go there, if she thought about the fact that her dad wouldn't be the one to walk her down the aisle she would lose it. She was thankful to have Cassie's dad to give her away. Mike Reagan had been like a second father to her all of her life and he would be there for her today. Cassie's folks and Holly's parents had been best friends. They had been tight since their high school days and their children had always been raised like cousins. The families did everything together. It was a natural thing for the Reagan's to take Holly in to live with them after her parents' death.

Holly sat on the edge of Rosa's bathtub as she fought off the feelings of emptiness that tried to worm their way into her heart. A single tear fell onto her lap. *I can't do this. I can't let these memories ruin my wedding day. Mom and Dad would want me to be happy and I know they are here with me in Spirit.* She took a deep breath and dabbed at her eyes with the handkerchief Cassie's mom had gifted her. *I'm ready.* With a twirl, Holly opened the door and walked out to the patio.

The band began to play the wedding march as Cassie's father took Holly's arm. Down the aisle they walked toward Joseph who stood beaming at them. He couldn't stop smiling. He felt like the luckiest guy alive.

The two exchanged vows that they had written for each other, with the priest from Rosa's church officiating. The Nolans were there in the front row.

They had fallen in love with Joseph when they first met him at the hos-pital just before Holly's release. As far as they were concerned, Holly was like a daughter so Joseph would be their adopted son-in-law. Harry reached for Dottie's hand, and gave it a little squeeze. They smiled at each other as they listened to the young couple pledge their troth.

After the rite, the celebrating began with a variety of appetizers followed by a buffet full of Rosa's specialties including bruschetta, penne pasta with cherry tomatoes, beef rolls with ricotta and mascarpone, eggplant with zucchini and Parmesan, a fruit punch for children, and another punch for the adults, made with Galliano, Aperol, and Prosecco.

The band began to play their first set, proving that they were quite versatile even though they were known mostly for the Celtic music they played each year at the Arizona Renaissance Festival. For their first dance together as man and wife, Holly, and Joseph chose an instrumental version of a song that Holly proclaimed 'their song' the first time she heard it on the radio: Christina Perri's *A Thousand Years*.

As the night wore on, the music seemed to get louder, as did the guests. Holly and Joseph were having a wonderful time, while at the same time they were getting anxious to begin their honeymoon. The first night they would be staying in a suite at a beautiful hotel downtown. The next day they would be flying to Cancun for a week's stay at a beachside resort.

They looked forward to snorkeling, sightseeing, and swimming with dolphins, but most of all they looked forward to spending time alone. The couple began saying their good-byes, with all of the guests bidding them goodnight, and bestowing their well wishes.

Cassie needed a break from the dance-floor where she had been practicing her moves. She sat at the first table she came to, which happened to be the table where Rosa was sitting, sipping at her third glass of punch. As Cassie took a seat across the table, Rosa gave her a nod.

This unconventional woman was Holly's best friend, and Rosa figured it was time she accepted the fact. As Cassie sat down, another couple at the table was just leaving. They were friends of Joseph's that Cassie didn't know.

The woman said, "I think fate brought those two together."

Her male companion answered in a flirtatious manner "Am I *your* fate?"

Laughing, she took his arm as they left by way of the side gate.

Cassie pondered the idea of fate as she reached for the bottle of wine, one of many that graced the tables. She poured herself a glass, and then decided to strike up a conversation with Rosa. The two had behaved like fans on opposing teams long enough.

"So, Mrs. Romero, what do you think? Was it fate that brought Holly and Joseph together?"

"Divine Providence, or the Wheel of Chance? The church would say that God's will is the natural order of things." So the conversation began.

"I believe in karma. I think that whatever we put out into the Universe comes back to us threefold. So, I suppose that we all create our own fate by the course of action we choose." Cassie spoke matter-of-factly.

"God cannot be set aside, though I agree that we should all be responsible for our own actions. Ultimately, it is God that knows what is best for us." Rosa retorted.

They agreed that folklore, including Italian tradition, gave fate a huge role in the destiny of mankind and generally personified that unseen power as three female figures who directed the fortunes of mere mortals. So, although they were in accord on various points, they couldn't come to terms with the idea that Holly and Joseph were somehow fated to be together.

As they talked, and drank more wine, their voices became louder, attracting attention from the remaining guests.

Mona, Cassie's date for the evening and partner for the last several months, came to the table from the kitchen where she was pitching in with the clean-up. She tapped Cassie on the shoulder.

"It's getting late. Maybe we should finish, call it a night."

"Sure hon. Thanks for the hospitality, Rosa." Cassie extended her hand.

Rosa took Cassie's hand and gave it a firm shake. There was no doubt that the two women were still posturing like mother wildcats looking out for their cubs. If asked, neither woman would be able to explain why they sensed danger whenever the other was around. They also couldn't rationally explain why the union of Holly and Joseph felt, for lack of a better term, 'ill-fated.'

When Holly and Joseph reached the hotel, they marveled at the beauty of the suite. Red rose petals were strewn across the extra-large king-sized bed. Satin sheets were turned back, and chocolates set upon the pillows. A large towel-art swan sat at the foot of the bed.

The mini bar was well stocked; flower arrangements were placed on every surface. A large fruit basket, a tray of cheeses with an assortment of crackers, and a large ice bucket holding a bottle of champagne sat on the coffee table in the adjacent sitting area.

In the large bathroom was a huge Jacuzzi tub which, like the bed, was also adorned with rose petals. On the back side was a row of candles, and in the corner a bottle of wine with two plastic wine glasses. It seemed that the hotel had thought of everything.

Joseph untied his tie and tossed it aside. He took off his jacket and draped it over a chair. He had wanted to peel that off all night. Dressing up in a suit and tie was not something he did that often, and he was glad of it.

"Why don't you get comfy and come over here." Joseph winked sitting on the side of the bed.

"I'm working on it," Holly called from where she stood at the bathroom door. She smiled back at him as she closed the door behind her. She sat on the edge of the large tub, unbuckling her high-heeled sandals, kicking them off, and wiggling her toes. Rising, she unzipped the lacey gown allowing it to slide off her shoulders down to the floor.

Looking in the mirror, she sized up her appearance. Her face was a bit flushed; strands of hair had escaped from her up-do. She continued to undress, removing her half-slip, nylons, bra, and panties. It was rare these days that she looked at herself naked.

Since the accident, she had developed a keen sense of modesty. This surprised everyone, not to mention herself. Before the accident, she had been perfectly okay with wearing a bikini to the pool. Now she felt a little embarrassed wearing a pair of mid-thigh length shorts. She appraised her body as if looking at it for the first time, just as she knew Joseph would soon be doing.

Fighting the urge to criticize the woman in the mirror, she took note of the changes in her body since the accident. Removing the clips that held her hair in place, she realized how long her hair was now, falling down to her mid-back. It was wavy from being pinned up, and felt silky against her bare skin.

She had also put on a little weight. Though she continued to work out, she did so sporadically. Her breasts were fuller, her tummy less toned, her hips more rounded. It was a sexier look, she supposed. She blushed, then turned from the mirror toward the Jacuzzi and began to fill the giant tub.

Tonight would be her second deflowering. Because of her newfound conservatism, she had put Joseph off when he tried to initiate sex, telling him that she wanted to wait until after the wedding. It didn't make good sense to her. Her mind couldn't descry a logical reason for her decision.

She loved Joseph and was wildly attracted to him. She had been sexually active since her senior year in high school, when she had fallen for her first love, Kevin. Joseph wasn't happy about it, but he agreed to tough it out, because there wasn't much of anything he wouldn't do for her, and because he didn't have much choice.

Joseph lay back on the bed waiting. She was taking a long time. He wondered if she were nervous. It was both frustrating and titillating that she had kept him at arm's length for this long. He longed to hold her, to be a part of her in all ways.

Just thinking about it made him feel extremely constricted in the tight dress slacks of his rented suit. He stood up and began to undress. He unbuttoned the long sleeved dress shirt and pulled it off with some difficulty; the arms of the shirt were snug across his biceps. He undid his belt buckle, whipping his belt off, snapping it in the air like a lion tamer. He tossed it across the room.

Next, he unbuttoned and unzipped his slacks, sliding one leg at a time out of both the pants and the briefs beneath them. He stood nude next to the bed flexing his muscles. Looking down it seemed another muscle was flexing under its own power. *Feeling pretty cocky, aren't we Joe.* Laughing at his own attempt at a joke, Joseph pulled the covers down, sliding in between the sheets of the comfy bed. He waited for Holly.

Holly lit the candles and poured two glasses of wine. She noticed some complimentary bath salts sitting by the sink and added a sprinkle of the aromatic crystals to the steaming tub. She turned the knob near the door, the lights dimmed. *Perfect.* Opening the door slightly, standing at an angle she beckoned to Joseph with her index finger.

When he heard the bathroom door open, he rose up to see her standing there. Only half of her body was visible from where he was reclining. He sat up and swung his legs over the side of the bed. His eyes focused in on all of her, one curve at a time, as he took mental photos of her.

Nature had always been his subject of choice. Now it seemed that Holly's silhouette was the most stunning scenery he had ever laid eyes on. Joseph wasted no time in joining her behind the bathroom door.

She reached out for him and he slipped his arm around her waist, guiding her to the waiting whirlpool. Holly sat down in the tub, sinking into the inviting bath. Joseph stepped into the water; he sat down behind her and pulled her into his chest. He cupped her breasts firmly but gently in his hands.

As he pressed against her, she felt his excitement. Slowly he began exploring every inch of her, kissing her hands, her arms, lightly running his tongue along the supple flesh of her shoulder finally nestling in her neck. He nibbled the edge of her ear, triggering what felt like little sparks of electricity. This made Holly's entire body shudder with anticipation.

Joseph took this as a cue to continue. He maneuvered around to face her. Lowering his head, he suckled and fondled her breasts, inducing her nipples to stiffened points. Meticulously, he moved lower, lapping water around her belly, sending her into a fit of giggles.

"Need a little break do we?" Joseph laughed. He reached for a wine glass, which he handed to Holly. He took the other glass; they toasted their good fortune at finding one another.

The water in the tub was cooling even as their passion was heating up. Holly suggested that they move their lovemaking to the bedroom. Joseph rose and grabbed a towel. He threw it over his shoulder, and then reached out to help Holly from the Jacuzzi. They toweled each other off as they proceeded to the bed, where they slid into the silky satin of the sheets.

The luxury of the bedding enfolded them. Holly lay on the pillow where Joseph had been reclining earlier in the evening. She detected the scent of the cologne he was wearing, one she had purchased for him. The woman at the fragrance counter had touted that the essence would transport her outdoors to a wild place, where rosemary, sage, and sandalwood grew in the shadow of tall pines and oaks covered with moss.

It had seemed like an exaggerated sales pitch at the time, yet Holly found that the scent delivered everything promised. It was sensuous and earthy, fitting Joseph perfectly.

He scooped her into his arms and brought her close. She lay on her back beaming up at him. Continuing with the erotic foreplay, he pulled the sheets back. Sitting on his knees at Holly's feet, he began caressing and massaging them.

Lovingly, he placed her feet one at a time on either side of his thighs. Leaning forward, he ran his fingers, then his tongue, along the insides of her thighs eventually reaching her velvety mound. Joseph seemed to know exactly how to please her. Her body arched and shuddered over and over. As she reached one pinnacle of pleasure, another awaited her.

Into the early morning hours, they explored and experimented with their bodies until they were drained. Eventually they settled in to sleep for a few short hours before they would have to be up to catch their flight. As Joseph snuggled up behind Holly, he noticed that she was wearing her locket. He wondered if she had been wearing it all night and if so he was amazed that he hadn't seen it before.

Just as they both dozed off, Holly murmured, "Goodnight, Jonathan."

Instinctively, Joseph replied, "Goodnight, Emeline."

Chapter Twenty-Nine

The next morning, which came all too soon given their long night of love-making, neither Joseph nor Holly remembered their odd goodnights.

Their honeymoon was all they had hoped for, with days on the beach, nights spent exploring the fine restaurants and entertainment offered at their resort. The two spent a good portion of their savings between the wedding and the trip, so when they returned it was time to get down to business.

"Yeah, Dad, I got the job. It's going to be great because I can work from home so I can be flexible if Holly finds work in another state, and it will be a steady paycheck. The company provides images for outdoor and nature conservation websites."

Joseph listened as his parents swapped the phone back and forth between them, each congratulating him on his new position.

Holly sailed through the front door, making hand signals and dancing around obviously excited about something.

"I've got to run Dad. I think Holly needs something. Talk to you soon. Tell Mom goodbye for me."

Holly laughed. "They are going to think I'm a demanding shrew. I just wanted to tell you that I have big news, too. You know how I've been applying to all of these different agencies, and I've been hoping to get something here in Arizona, well.... I got on with the Bureau of Land Management!

"I don't start until the spring. The salary won't be great, and the work will be hard, but I will be out in nature, not stuck behind a desk." Holly was bouncing up and down. Joseph put his hands on her shoulders to calm her down. He gave her a big bear hug.

"Wow, that's great news. Where exactly are we going? Northern part of the state?"

"Yes, it's near Prescott in Yavapai County. And guess what? The job comes with a cabin for us to live in!"

"That's amazing; you said you always wanted to live in a cabin. Is it in the woods, like your dream house?" Joseph winked.

"As a matter of fact, it is."

"Let's celebrate. How about Thai food?"

"Sounds great." Holly picked up her purse from the chair where she had left it. Joseph pulled their jackets from the coat rack near the door and helped Holly into hers before putting on his own.

When Joseph opened the door, he heard carolers approaching from down the street. It reminded him that he hadn't decided on a gift for Holly. He wanted it to be something special because this would be their first Christmas together as a married couple. He pondered on what to get her as they got into the Jeep. *More to think about, great.*

Joseph's mind had been ping-ponging back and forth over jobs, family, and the upcoming move. *I wish Mom and Dad hadn't decided to retire from their trucking business just as I am leaving town. It's pretty ironic. At least they will be there for Nonna.* Joseph knew that his grandmother was going to miss him very much. He hoped she wouldn't blame Holly for dragging him away.

When March rolled around, Joseph and Holly packed a small U-Haul with their meager possessions, and off they went to begin their lives in the wilderness.

Their new home was on forest land. To get there, they had to follow a two-lane highway that led to a turn-off onto a very bumpy dirt road of about six miles, which eventually ended at the property line. A locked gate kept the public from the path leading to the house.

The cabin was made of stone. One side faced a winding creek. Wide stone steps led up to the one-story rectangular building. The walls were maybe two feet thick, made of large stones cemented together. The roof was metal and overhung large lodge pole beams.

The interior layout offered a large living area, kitchen, and two bedrooms with a small bathroom between them. There was pine flooring, built in bookcases on two walls, plus a granite fireplace in the main room. Joseph and Holly loved it.

"I think I'll hang some of my photos over here." Joseph held a level in one hand and a hammer in the other.

"Don't forget to hang my needlepoint while you are in the mood to hang things."

"Will do."

Chapter Thirty

The days, weeks, and months seemed to fly by. Holly and Joseph stayed very busy working, building their careers and enjoying their free time together. Over time, Holly found that her bouts of confusion, and her odd thoughts, were happening less often. As she began to feel more like herself, or at least more comfortable in her own skin, everyone around her fell back into their routines.

Cassie and Mona, her date for Holly's and Joseph's wedding, began to see more and more of each other. After several months of dating, they decided to move in together, renting an apartment in Flagstaff. Cassie had always wanted to own her own business, so when her favorite pizza place went up for sale, Cassie saw her opportunity. Mona came on board as her business partner; they bought the place and began renovations to turn the outdated restaurant into a swank new bistro.

It was Holly's misadventure that had brought Cassie and Mona together in the first place. Mona had been working in the hospital when Holly had her accident. She sparked Cassie's interest right away, and they flirted back and forth until Holly's release, when Cassie had asked Mona out for lunch.

Following Joseph's and Holly's marriage, Mona decided to quit her nursing job in Tucson. She moved to Flagstaff to be with Cassie. Soon after, she took a job at a local clinic where she would continue to work up until the bistro was a moneymaking proposition.

Back in Tucson, Rosa Romero was adjusting to the absence of her favorite grandson. Having her son and daughter-in-law close at hand was wonderful. Most days their presence kept her mind off Joseph. There were days, though, when she would pick up his photo from the shelf where it now sat in the very place where Holly's locket had lain, at the feet of the Fates. She would hold it in her hand, and say a silent prayer for him, then kiss the photo and set it back on the shelf. This little ritual helped her to feel connected to her Tesoro even though he was miles away.

Her concerns with Holly and the locket lessened as she came to know and love the young woman. She laughed at herself for getting worked up over nothing. She regretted that her relationship with Holly started off on the wrong foot.

Chapter Thirty-One

Before they knew it, Holly and Joseph were celebrating a third wedding anniversary. Holly was happily enjoying a new promotion. The post meant
a higher salary as well as more benefits. Joseph had started his own Internet
company that hosted photographers' portfolios. He also provided a stock photography catalog for buyers and professional photographers. The inventory
specialized in nature, travel and outdoor photography. His venture was really
taking off.

The pair began to consider parenthood. This was something they had both
looked forward to; their excitement at the prospect of a new baby was contagious. Friends and family anxiously awaited an announcement. The first question that anyone would ask when they saw or talked to either Holly or Joseph
was, "Any big news yet?"

It was June when Holly began to feel the first signs of a pregnancy. "I'm a
little queasy, and I can't tolerate the smell of some foods, other than that, I feel
fine." Holly sat on the porch swing that Joseph had just installed as she chatted
by phone with Cassie.

"I can't wait to go shopping for this kid. I'm a sucker for tiny clothes,
especially shoes." Cassie squealed.

"Now then, don't get carried away. We won't know whether it's a girl or a
boy for a few more weeks."

"Are you going to deliver at a hospital, or birthing center, or what?"

"Actually, since our cabin is so far from the nearest hospital, we are going
to use the services of a local midwife. The thought of giving birth in the comfort of our own home sounds wonderful to me."

"What if something goes wrong?"

"We have a doctor and hospital lined up if we need them. Luckily, the nurse-midwife we found works closely with a local obstetrician. You would like this woman. Allison Grey is her name. She is forty-something; she's a small woman with a big heart. She is very professional. Her years of experience really show. She is calm, comforting, and caring. Her bedside manner is great and I'm thrilled to have found her."

"Great, it sounds like you have it all worked out. I'm sure everything will go smoothly. Keep me posted. I'll be window shopping for my new niece or nephew."

"Bye Cassie. I'll call you later in the week."

"Okay, bye."

Family and friends were all delighted for Holly and Joseph. They all agreed that they would be wonderful parents. Rosa began crocheting a baby blanket in a rainbow pattern fit for either a boy or a girl. She fought off the urge to pull out her cards, to do a reading for the baby. She didn't think her old heart could take it if anything unusual happened or if the reading were in any way negative.

Cassie, on the other hand, was quick to lay out a Tarot spread for the new addition to the Romero clan. Afterwards, she was unsure of her decision. *Unsettling* was the word she would have used to describe the feeling she experienced after scrutinizing the cards.

The significator, the card which represented the child in the reading, was the Moon, the wild card of the Major Arcana. Of course, there were many ways to interpret the card, yet, generally speaking, it meant that the person was - or in the case of the unborn, would be - moody, secretive, sensitive, and a little irrational.

He or she could either wander through life battling addictions, wallowing in depression, alienating friends and family with wild, antisocial behavior, or get focused and go through it purposefully. In this case, the child should take up painting, writing, poetry, or some other creative endeavor, where they could transform all he or she saw and felt into something beautiful. It looked like a roller coaster ride ahead for Holly and Joseph if this little one had the traits of the Moon.

Joseph could hardly contain his excitement over the impending birth. He worried for Holly's safety at work; he hovered over her when she was home.

"Joseph, your concern is admirable, but you're smothering me."

"Sorry, I just don't want you to overdo it."

Holly found his actions charming, even though there were days when she wished he had a job outside the cabin to go to. *He will be an amazing father.* Holly smiled to herself as she envisioned Joseph with a baby strapped to his back.

The baby was due very close to Holly's birthday. She thought this would be her best ever birthday present. She wanted to be surprised by her gift. So when it came time for an ultrasound she and Joseph agreed that they didn't want to know the sex of the child. Either way they would be pleased as long as the baby was healthy.

Chapter Thirty-Two

It was early morning, the twenty-third of December. The thermometer on the windowsill said it was twenty-three degrees. Joseph was building a fire in the stone fireplace when Holly yelped.

"I think it's time." She stood in the kitchen doorway with one hand over her round tummy. Standing there, Joseph thought she looked like a little girl hiding a basketball under her shirt. Her hair hung in braids behind her ears. She wore a pair of sweat pants, cartoon character slippers, and Joseph's tee shirt stretched over her Buddha belly.

The twinges that had kept her from sleeping with comfort the night before were now coming with a regularity and increasing strength that she felt sure was more than the Braxton-Hicks contractions that she had been feeling in the past couple of weeks.

Joseph dropped the log he was holding. He stared open mouthed at her. Coming to his senses, he said, "I'll call Allison."

"Okay. I think I'll sit down here by the fire." Holly indicated a rocking chair with a high back. She waddled over to it and sat down.

Joseph snatched his cell phone from the kitchen counter. He began making phone calls. The first call was to Allison, who assured him that she would be there soon. This being a first baby, she felt sure that there were hours of waiting ahead; still, she wanted to be there to help coach Holly through her labor. The tote holding her necessities was stowed in her car, ready in anticipation of Joseph's call.

After phoning Allison, Joseph called his parents, Nonna, and Cassie. They, in turn, began calling others until pretty much everyone who knew the couple had been notified of the impending birth.

Holly sat in front of the fireplace as the fire came to life. Her hands were cold. She rubbed them together, wishing the fire would start emitting some heat. Joseph brought her a blanket, draping it over her lap. He hefted a footstool from next to the sofa, set it in front of the chair, and gently placed her feet on it.

As she sat there, she gazed out the window at the gleam of frost covering the surface of everything. It sparkled on the hoods of their vehicles, the grass, trees, and the fence posts. Their entire yard looked like a glittery fairyland, a perfect day to be born.

All day, into the evening, Joseph and Allison, took turns with Holly. They played cards until Holly no longer could concentrate on the game. They rubbed her back as they encouraged her to breathe. For Holly, the day seemed to drag on as the agony of her pains increased.

Joseph grew progressively more nervous pacing up and down, then circumnavigating the freshly decorated Christmas tree as he munched on peppermint bark and chocolate chip cookies. Finally, after watching this spectacle for several minutes Holly shouted "For the love of God, *sit down!*"

Joseph promptly sat on the sofa. He picked up a magazine from the coffee table, looking through the pages, not at all interested in the subject matter.

Allison suggested that they all try watching a Christmas movie on her laptop. This proved to be a good distraction for the time being, though by the time the film ended Holly's labor was in full swing. Allison assisted Holly to the pullout sofa that had been set up for her delivery. When she examined her, she determined that the time had come. Holly was ready to begin pushing.

Since Joseph's early morning phone calls, there had been a lot of not-so-patient waiting among those concerned with the welfare of the little family. Cassie checked her watch every few minutes while working at the restaurant.

Further south, in Tucson, Rosa, along with Joseph's parents, spent the day shopping for groceries and wrapping Christmas gifts. They talked non-stop about the coming grand/great-grandchild, their own little Christmas miracle.

The sun had just gone to bed for the night, leaving a pale glow on the horizon, when Holly's last shriek gave way to the cry of a newborn babe.

"It's a girl. She looks perfect." Allison broadcast as she allowed Joseph to cut the cord. She looked the child over, took a quick listen with the stethoscope hanging from her neck, and placed the child on Holly's chest.

Joseph leaned in to kiss his wife "Hey, you are amazing. Look at how beautiful she is." He beamed at his new daughter. Holly was exhausted but felt fabulous all at the same time. A rush of tears escaped her eyes, streaming down her face. Joseph looked concerned.

"It's okay, these are happy tears." Holly smiled up at him. "She is beautiful." She snuggled the baby who had already latched on and was blissfully nursing.

"So what is her name?" Allison asked as she filled out the necessary paperwork. Holly looked at Joseph, who pulled a list from his pocket.

"Well, we had it narrowed down to two names for a girl and two for a boy. The girl's were Amelia and Amanda. Which one seems right to you?"

Holly thought about it as she looked down at the tiny bundle. "Neither one seems to fit her. What do you think?"

Joseph knelt to the child's level "Hello there Amelia." *Maybe not.* "Hello there, Amanda." He looked at Holly again. "I don't know. You are right, neither name seems like hers."

As she held the baby, something in the room magnetized Holly's gaze. A gorgeous holiday bouquet sat on the kitchen table. The flowers had been delivered the previous day. They were a gift from the Nolans. The vase contained red roses, white lilies, and Alstroemenia, along with fresh greens. Tiny red, silver and pearl ornaments sparkled among the flowers.

"That's it." Holly exclaimed. "Her name should be a Christmas botanical, just like mine. After all, she and I almost share a birthday."

Holly was so animated; obviously delighted with her decision that Joseph had to agree. "That sounds perfect. So what specifically are you thinking?"

Holly mentally ran through a short list of possibilities. "I'm thinking Lily, like the ones in that arrangement." She pointed toward the flowers. "Do you like it, hon?"

Joseph said the name out loud. "Lily." The baby stopped nursing, letting out a little hiccup. "I think she likes it." Joseph chuckled. "Lily it is."

Holly piped up, "Lily Rose Romano." Allison nodded. She filled the name in on the birth certificate.

Now that Lily was through with her first meal, Holly suggested that Joseph have his turn to hold her. He gladly scooped her up, holding her against his chest. She was so small in his arms. A rush of fatherly pride and protectiveness welled up inside of him. He sat down in the rocker. He began to sway, Lily lying vertically on his lap. The rhythmic movement prompted Joseph to begin humming. The humming turned to song.

"The maid shakes her head, on her lips lays her fingers. Steals up from the seat, longs to go and yet lingers. A frightened glance turns to her drowsy grandmother. Puts one foot on the stool, spins the wheel with the other.

"Merrily, cheerily, noisily, whirring, swings the wheel, spins the wheel, while the foot's stirring. Sprightly and lightly and airily ringing, sounds the sweet voice of the young maiden singing."

"That's a lovely tune. What is it? I don't recognize that song" Allison wanted to know.

"I guess I learned it when I was a kid. I looked it up online because I don't think I ever knew the title. Its' called *The Spinning Wheel*. According to the sources I checked, it is an old Irish ballad written by the poet John Francis Waller in the mid-1800s.

"I have Holly to thank for bringing this song back for me. It just popped into my head back when she almost drowned in that flash flood. Holly told you about that, didn't she?"

"Yes, she did. Lucky for her that you came along when you did. Lucky for you as well, I would say." She smiled.

"We are one very lucky pair." Joseph grinned at Holly.

Allison continued as she packed her bags. "An old Irish ballad is a nice tribute to Lily's heritage on her mom's side. I'm sure you know an Italian tune or two. You have a nice voice, by the way."

"Thanks. I do know an Italian song or two." Joseph thought of the songs Rosa and his mother sang to him. The first that came to mind given the season was *La Befana*. He sang.

"La Befana vien di notte, con le scarpe tutte rotte. Ai bambini piccolini, lascie tanti chocolatini. Ai bambini cativoni, lascie cenere e carbone.

"Italian legend has it that La Befana is an old woman in tattered clothing, a witch who delivers gifts to children on Epiphany, the day that the Wise Men purportedly delivered gifts to the baby Jesus.

"La Befana is much like Santa Claus. She gives nice gifts like candy and toys to good children, coal to naughty ones. She travels by broom. The English translation of this version is something like this. He crooned.

"The Befana comes at night, in worn out shoes. To the little children, she leaves a lot of little chocolates. To the bad little children, she leaves ashes and coal."

Then he said, "The rhyme and the song vary depending on the part of Italy you visit, although the legend is pretty much the same."

Chapter Thirty-Three

She sat on the braided rug, her toys scattered around her. Lost in thought, Lily was unusually quiet and still for a customarily active four-year-old. Again, the dream came last night.

It tortured her more and more frequently. Some of the time she was afraid to sleep for fear that she would have the dream again. Her parents were aware that something was bothering her. They knew she had trouble sleeping. Her mother asked if nightmares were the problem. Lily didn't know what qualified as a nightmare.

If nightmares were scary dreams, this was a nightmare. If she told her mother the truth, she would want details. Lily couldn't tell her much. The dream was always about her, her mom. There was another woman in the dream, as well. A woman with long dark hair washing clothes in a river, a large black bird perched on her shoulder.

She said the same thing, repeating it incessantly. "Your clothes are almost clean, dearie." It wasn't a frightening statement, yet it made Lily feel uneasy. The part of the dream that scared Lily the most was when her mother also showed up in the dream at the river's edge. The water was always running very fast and very hard. It made a loud roaring noise.

At the bank of this waterway, her mother held a doll. She tossed the doll into the water, turning with a scowl she glared at Lily. As Lily looked back at her mother in the dream, Holly's face would change. Her features would transform until she wore the face of another woman.

Her hair and eye color changed too. When the metamorphosis was complete, a woman with blond hair and violet blue eyes had replaced her mother.

This woman seemed like her mother too. It didn't make any sense. Lily's four-year-old mind assuredly couldn't sort it out.

The dream left Lily feeling depressed. It gave her bad thoughts about her mother. Her stomach hurt. The emotions were not something she could have expressed even if she had wanted to. She began to withdraw, especially when she was at home alone with Holly.

Her daddy was in the middle of a big assignment with a magazine taking photos of animals. Lily wished that he would come home soon, that he would never leave again. She trusted her father in a way that she could never trust her mother.

Holly sat at the kitchen table drinking her coffee and going through the mail. She looked over at Lily sitting on the floor, apparently in a daze. The little girl had hardly moved for a solid ten minutes. What was she daydreaming about?

Holly was really worried about her daughter. The nightmares were getting worse. Lily wasn't getting enough sleep. Holly racked her brain trying to come up with a reason why the girl would have all of these bad dreams.

Nothing traumatic had occurred within the household. Violent TV shows were not the cause because they didn't have a television. They only allowed her to watch carefully selected videos on the computer. Usually Holly accompanied Lily at pre-school, and there was nothing negative going on there.

The most recent development was Lily's attitude toward Holly. She kept her distance as much as possible from her mother, as if she didn't trust her. When Joseph was at home, Lily would follow him around like his shadow.

If Joseph asked her to do something, she did it right away, without complaint. If Holly asked her to do the same thing, she was met with defiance. Lily began to have tantrums around Holly, started talking back, being sassy. With Joseph, she was a perfect little angel. This marked preference for her father sparked some anger and a bit of jealousy in Holly that surprised her. It made her feel ashamed.

Holly set down her cup, picked up her cell phone, and walked out to the porch. She tried Cassie's number, hoping she would pick up. Lately, it had been hard to reach her friend; she often ended up leaving a voice mail message. This time Cassie answered.

"Hi ho. What's new?" Cassie sounded chipper.

"I don't know, I guess I just called to vent."

"Trouble in paradise?" Cassie joked. She didn't think that was likely. Holly and Joseph got along almost too well.

"Sort of. I'm just at my wits' end with Lily."

"Not that sweet cherub. Getting into mischief is she?" Cassie couldn't picture the little girl she knew behaving badly. She smiled to herself envisioning Lily wearing the purple dress she had bought her, bouncing around the room as she pretended to be a fairy princess. Lily, with her rosy cheeks, big brown eyes and long, wavy, chocolate colored hair. She was one cute kid.

Holly agreed that Lily was indeed cherubic most of the time, especially with Cassie, whom she adored. Holly went on to explain to Cassie about the dreams, along with her concerns with Lily's behavior, attitude, and seeming defiance, all aimed at Holly herself.

Cassie didn't know what to make of it all. Holly might be over-reacting. The dreams did concern Cassie. According to Holly, Lily wouldn't say much about the dreams. Just that a scary lady was washing clothes in a river. Cassie asked Holly why Lily felt so frightened by the woman.

"She doesn't say. I asked her if the woman had a mean face. She said no. I asked if the lady tried to hurt her. She denied that as well."

Cassie pictured the woman washing clothes at the waterside. Her penchant for mythology overtook her thoughts. She visualized the image of Macha, an aspect of the Celtic triple Goddess collectively known as the Morrigan. The Washer at the Ford is said to be one aspect of Her.

She appears to those about to die. She is commonly shown washing bloody clothes at a river ford; when approached, she tells the enquirer the clothes are theirs. Like the *bean sidhe* – the banshee - whom she is believed to be related to, she is an omen of death.

Cassie felt a cold shiver prickling over her shoulder blades. Holly, on the other end of the phone, was waiting for a response to a question that Cassie had not heard. "So, should I call or not?"

"Call who?" Cassie sounded distracted.

"If this is a bad time, I …."

"No, no, repeat what you just said. I let my mind wander. I was trying to figure out what was bothering Lily."

Cassie wasn't about to tell Holly about Macha. It was just an eerie coincidence, nothing more. Cassie brushed off the feeling of gloom that tried to invade her subconscious.

"I asked you if you thought I should call Joseph. Even though he calls us every evening to talk and to tell Lily goodnight, I think I need to talk to him now."

"So call him already. Why are you even asking me?"

"Okay, I guess I just needed some encouragement. Thanks for listening." Holly always felt better when she talked to Cassie, no matter what the problem.

"Could Lily's pediatrician shed some light on the nightmares? Maybe even help with her behavior issues?"

"I did call her. She sent me some information to read on both subjects. I tried a few parenting tips, plus I googled until I'm all searched out. Nothing I've tried has helped. If only Joseph was home, it would be so much easier to deal with Lily. This is his last big shoot for this project, so when he gets back maybe we can all go back to normal."

"There you have it! I think you might have just stumbled onto the answer. Lily is just acting out because she holds you somehow responsible for her father's absence. Maybe she thinks you are a slave driver. You know, get out there, take pictures." Cassie was giggling now, and it was contagious.

Holly laughed. "You are certifiable. Thanks for lightening my mood for me. You actually might have a point. Lily might just be unhappy with Joseph gone. They are as thick as thieves."

"I'm going to let you go. You had better go see what she is up to. I'll talk to you later."

"Take care. Don't fret - you will get all wrinkly. Bye."

"Bye, Cass." Holly let out a sigh.

Turning toward the front window, she peered in. Lily remained on the rug, her position and posture unchanged.

Holly didn't call Joseph. She didn't know what to say. Every time she rehearsed what she wanted to say it sounded ridiculous as she said it out loud to herself. So, she waited.

At the end of the month, Joseph came home. Holly and Lily were glad to have him back. He was just as thrilled to be back home.

The shoot had been enlivening, providing a new zeal for his web business. His enthusiasm lifted Holly's mood. Lily's dreams tapered off, and she began to act like the Lily, she had been before the onset of the nightmares. Holly was relieved; it looked as though Cassie had nailed it.

Months passed without incident. Spring came and with it, the first thaw in the mountains. Joseph, along with a couple of friends, began planning for a three-years-running, now annual, camping trip. A long weekend of hiking, exploring - and for Joseph, photo opportunities.

Holly planned a girls' weekend. The first night she invited a friend and her five-year-old daughter to come out to their house for a sleepover. She planned games for the kids, to be followed by pizza and movies. The next day she would take Lily on a picnic.

Friday night, Holly's friend Elaine showed up with her daughter Emma. The girls went straight to Lily's small bedroom. They played while Holly and Elaine prepared the pizza. They must have been having a good time, judging from their laughter.

While the dough was rising for the homemade crust, the women brought out the board games. Lily and Emma voted for their favorites. As the pizza cooked, they managed to play through a couple of games, Lily won every time; Emma was a good sport. The pizza was delicious, and everyone enjoyed movies and popcorn until well past the girls' regular bedtime.

They all slept well, including Lily. In the morning, after a breakfast of French toast with fruit, Elaine helped Holly clean up the kitchen. Lily and Emma retreated to Lily's room to play with their action figures from the latest Disney movie.

"I'm going to throw a load of towels in the washer," Holly told Elaine as she gathered the hand towel and dishcloths they just finished using in the kitchen. She started for the bathroom, to collect the remaining dirty towels.

"Okay, I'll make us some fresh coffee. I want to try your new fancy one-cup-at-a-time coffee maker." Elaine heard Holly laughing at the comment. "What can I say? I'm easily amused."

"Will your Mommy let you come to my house later?" Emma asked Lily.

As Holly walked past Lily's room, she heard Emma's question. She also heard Lily's somewhat delayed answer.

"She had better let me. She owes me." Lily said it very matter-of-factly without emotion.

Holly stood motionless in the hallway.

In Lily's room, Emma shrugged her shoulders. Unable to understand her friend's comment, she went on playing, making up an alternate universe where stuffed elephants were best friends with dolphins, and tiny plastic warriors drove Lego cars into battle.

Holly wandered into the bathroom, picked up the strewn towels, and then went into the tiny laundry area. She loaded the machine, added soap and fabric softener, and pressed the start button. As she made her way back to the kitchen, she contemplated what she had heard.

It didn't seem like something a four year old would say. Where had Lily picked up something like that, and how would she know to use it appropriately in a sentence the way she had? Moreover, why would she say such a thing? *How do I owe her anything, I mean other than …. Of course I owe her a decent life. I gave her life. Damn. What … the … .*

"Elaine, if I told you that I just heard Lily say that I 'owe her,' what would you say?" Holly said in a hushed tone as she entered the room. She didn't want the kids to hear her.

"I would say that I think you probably either misheard her or she has been watching too much Showtime." Elaine smiled over her coffee cup.

"I'm pretty sure I heard her right. You know we don't have a TV, so cable channels can't be to blame." Holly wasn't smiling back. Elaine could see that she was really upset.

"Kids say the darnedest things. As a matter of fact, that was a TV show, one popular enough for a remake. Don't take it personally, or think too much about it." Elaine was doing her best to reassure Holly; still, she could see that it wasn't working. "I guess we should take off, let you do some mother-daughter bonding. You were going to go on a little hike and picnic today, right, just the two of you?"

"Mmm, yeah. I was going to take her over to that little meadow just beyond that stand of pines behind the house."

"I think she will love that. You'll see that some one-on-one time is all she wants from you." Elaine came to Holly's side and gave her a squeeze. Holly smiled and returned the hug.

The day was perfect for an outdoor excursion. It was cool enough for a light jacket because of a gentle breeze blowing down the side of the mountains. The peaks still had snow, though it was fast melting. The creeks would be running, and a few presumptuous wildflowers were already shooting up.

The sun shone brightly in the morning sky with just a few wispy clouds scattered across the blue canvas overhead. After waving good-bye to their friends, Holly and Lily went into the kitchen. They began to prepare their picnic.

Holly assembled all of the ingredients for sandwich making on the table. While she constructed their sandwiches, Lily went to the lower cabinet where the snack items were kept. She pulled out a container of trail mix. They packed fruit and bottles of water in a small cooler carefully stacking the sandwiches on top. During the preparation, Lily bounced around the room like a healthy, happy four year old, which delighted Holly and put her mind at ease.

They each donned a fleece hoodie and Holly chose a Mexican blanket from the closet to spread out under their picnic. Tossing in the sunscreen, as well as a small first aid kit, Holly felt ready for anything. She picked up her small backpack from the table near the front door, and shoved the last minute items into it. She felt around in the pack to see if she had her digital camera and found its case.

"It looks as if we have everything. Let's go."

"Can I take some of my toys?" Lily stood in the doorway of her room with a handful of playthings.

"Sure, just a couple. Don't forget we have to carry everything. Travel light."

"Okay, Mommy." Lily put the toys into her own small backpack, and wriggled into the straps.

They left the house, walked across the backyard and out the rear gate, following a timeworn path through the tall saffron-hued grasses. Lily skipped along, enjoying the warm sunlight. The picnic would be fun. Holly walked just behind Lily on the path. The scent of pine was heavy in the air; she breathed deeply savoring the fresh aroma.

With her mother following her lead, Lily sped up when she spotted the row of trees, which meant that their destination was just yards away. Something began to germinate in a dark corner of Lily's mind. She began to wonder if her mother were luring her to the meadow for some wicked purpose.

It made her angry when she had bad thoughts about her mother. Mommy was never mean; she loved her sooo much. Yet, these nagging thoughts kept creeping in. When the thoughts came, they made her do bad things, and say mean things. She took off at a dead run trying her hardest to outrun the confusion.

"Lily, don't go so fast," Holly shouted after her.

Lily wasn't listening. Holly broke into a jog. Just as Lily approached the trees, she panicked. It occurred to her that her mother might try to lead her the wrong way. Maybe she would lose her in the forest just like Hansel and Gretel's stepmother had done in the book. She would tell her daddy that she ran away.

Daddy might never find her; this scared her. She would hide from Mommy; go home when she knew that Daddy would be back from his camping trip. If she could make it to the other side of the grassy area known as The Meadow, she would be under cover of a thickly forested hillside. She bolted in that direction.

When Lily picked up her pace so did Holly. She didn't know why Lily was in such a big hurry. This was supposed to be a peaceful, relaxing day; it felt more like running a marathon. When Lily's pink hoodie bounced beyond their destination into the cover of the woods, Holly felt uneasy.

"Lily, come here. Let's set up our picnic." She tried to sound calm. Lily was nowhere to be seen, so Holly called toward the last place she had spotted the girl.

"Don't hide, silly. I might start without you." Again she enticed. Lily did not respond.

Holly left the blanket and her backpack on the grass, and ran for the trees. She called and cajoled. Still, no response, no sign of Lily. Maybe if she went back to the blanket, and sat there for a few minutes, pretending to ignore her, Lily might tire of the game and come out.

Holly strolled back to the items laying in the grass, picked up the blanket, shook it out and laid it flat on top of the grass. She unzipped her backpack, removed the food and drinks, and then took a swig of water from her bottle.

At the bottom of her backpack was a paperback novel that she had started but never finished. She found the tiny bookmark where she had left off. She made an effort to read a page. All the while she kept one eye on the edge of the woodlands where Lily had disappeared.

It was scary inside the wooded area. The sunlight barely made it through the dense canopy. In the shadows, Lily watched as her mother spread the blanket and sat down. The tiny voice in her head that nagged at her constantly now spoke up.

"See, she doesn't care about you. You could be hurt or dead. Attacked by bears or kidnapped by mean men camping in the woods." When the voice piped up, Lily's mood always turned hostile. *How dare she abandon me? I'll show her.* Lily ran further into the trees.

Holly couldn't sit still. Ignoring Lily was obviously not working. It had been ten minutes since she sat down, trying to wait out the girl's game of hide-and-seek. She picked up the picnic items and threw the blanket over her shoulder with her backpack.

Jogging toward the tree line, she hailed loudly, "Lily!" There was no sign of the child as Holly scanned the timbers. Her heart raced as she tried to stave off the panic that gripped her.

Lily curled up next to a tall pine. She pulled out her pink plush kitty from her backpack. She held the small soft toy to her chest and waited. The voice in her head had gone silent; fear had replaced the anger at her mother. Mommy was all she wanted. She was too scared to move for fear that she would go the wrong direction. She might end up even further away from her mother and the meadow.

Holly frantically called for Lily as she navigated further into the woods. She stopped to turn on a phone app that tracked her movements. The last thing she wanted was to lose track of where she was and end up lost. She had to be able to get herself and Lily safely back to the meadow. Time seemed to be passing quickly, shadows were lengthening, and she had to find Lily before the sun dropped any lower.

Lily was getting hungry; her tummy was making growling noises. Mommy had all the food. She wished she hadn't run away. She really wished she hadn't gone so far into the forest. Strange sounds startled her. *Just birds, that's all.* Soon after, she heard a sound that made her feel warm and safe, her mother's voice. It sounded unusually raspy, but it was Mommy's voice. Lily called back to her "Mommy, I'm here."

Holly heard the response; she tumbled toward the direction of the call. "Lily." They called back and forth. When they saw each other, they ran into an embrace. Holly's sense of relief was overpowering. She burst into tears, as did Lily. Holly picked up her little girl, checked her phone for direction, and then hiked back toward the grassy field.

Once clear of the trees, Holly sat Lily down. They walked back to the house. The afternoon was almost over and neither felt like picnicking. Not much was said until they reached home. Holly was too emotionally drained to talk to Lily about her stunt.

She fixed them dinner; silently they ate. As Holly readied Lily for bed, she asked her why she had run away from her. Lily couldn't explain. Mommy and Daddy could sort of understand when she told them about the nightmares, but the voice in her head was something her four-year-old self and vocabulary could not articulate. So she just said, "I don't know."

The voice, which Lily mentally referred to as The Mad Lady, began to take over her thoughts randomly about the same time as the nightmares started. The lady was angry at Mommy. Mommy had taken something from her.

Lily knew that the lady was somehow a part of herself; she wasn't *other*. Lily thought back. She couldn't think of anything that Mommy ever took from her, except the scissors. That was normal stuff. Her friend's mothers did that sort of thing too. Yet this inner voice told her to seek revenge for an unknown wrong. The angry outbursts and defiance were emotions that Lily seemed to have little control over. Lily softly cried herself to sleep.

Holly's frustration level was sky high. Joseph would be home tomorrow around noon. She couldn't wait. She missed him. This time she *had* to discuss Lily's increasing misbehavior. It was more than simply acting out, she was sure of it. If Lily kept this up, she would force Joseph into never leaving her. That would reward her antics by giving her exactly what it seemed she wanted, her father.

Chapter Thirty-Four

Sunday morning Holly was up before dawn. Her night had been fraught with restlessness and worry. She stumbled into the bathroom; she hoped that a hot shower with some eucalyptus body wash would wake her up.

She took off her pajamas and removed the locket from her neck. The only time she took it off was to shower. She set it on the counter next to the sink, in a little porcelain dish, as she always did. After her shower, she threw on a terry bathrobe before she went back to her bedroom to dress.

After putting herself together for the day, she headed to the kitchen to make coffee. When she heard Lily stirring, she started a batch of pancakes.

She called to Lily. When she got no response, she went to check on her. Lily sat on the bed surrounded by her favorite dolls and a couple of stuffed animals. She didn't acknowledge Holly when she stepped through the door. "Lily I made some pancakes. I put chocolate chips in half of them just for you."

Lily turned her head. She glared at Holly. "I'm not hungry."

"Well, you need to eat something, so come to the table now," Holly demanded with as stern a voice as she could muster. Lily had worn her down, there was no denying it.

Holly went back to the kitchen and sat down with her second cup of coffee. A couple of minutes later, Lily came shuffling into the room wearing her fluffy blue slippers, holding a doll under one arm.

"Chocolate chip pancakes, yummy." She sat in her usual seat and smiled at Holly. "Can I have three?"

Holly didn't know how a four year old was able to play such mind games. She put three pancakes on a plate. "Three is a lot. Are you sure you can eat this much? You said you weren't hungry." Holly pulled out a drawer retrieving a fork and a butter knife.

Lily tossed her doll onto the floor. "I changed my mind," she said flatly.

Joseph arrived as scheduled. As soon as Holly heard his truck approaching, she ran outside to meet him. The truck bed was full of firewood. "We got bored, so we decided to gather up some dead limbs, and it escalated." He gave Holly a hug and kiss. "I missed you."

"You don't know how much I missed you." Holly whispered back. Lily now ran from the house. She grabbed Joseph around the legs. "Daddy, I'm so glad you're home. I love you." He picked her up and swung her around. She screamed in delight. With Daddy home, the voice would quiet down. She and Mommy would be okay.

That afternoon while Lily took a nap, an uncommon occurrence since her fourth birthday, Holly sat down next to Joseph, who was parked on the couch browsing the Internet on his tablet. "We need to talk about Lily." She sounded serious.

Joseph put the device down next to his camera bag. He saw her concern in her expression and heard it in the tone of her voice. She explained all of her worries. She told him what Lily was saying and doing, about her misbehavior, and about the anger that Lily displayed toward her.

Joseph listened. He waited until she had finished before making a comment. "Why on Earth did you wait so long to tell me this?"

"I thought you wouldn't believe me, or take it seriously. She doesn't pull this stuff with you. I guess I thought you would take her side." It sounded bad; she knew it, which was why she ended up waiting this long to say something.

"Really, Holly I can't believe you kept this to yourself." Joseph jumped up. He began pacing. He shoved his fingers into his pockets to keep from expressing himself with his hands.

"I'll sit her down and have a chat with her when she wakes up. Kids go through stages. Maybe she is going through some sort of Oedipus complex thing. Girls sometimes idolize their fathers and are jealous of their mothers. If that's what is going on, and if I remember correctly from Psych one-oh-one, she will grow out of it."

"I suppose that's possible … but in the meantime, how do I handle it? I think we should take her to somebody." Holly felt better discussing the problem. Keeping her concerns from Joseph had caused added stress.

"You mean you think she needs a shrink? You're the one that said you hated being analyzed. We would all be put under the microscope." Joseph balked at the idea. "I'll talk to her. Some of the deeds you think she is doing … well, I don't see how a four year old could be so calculating."

"Joseph, are you calling me a liar?" Holly tried to keep her voice steady and low so as not to wake Lily.

"No, of course not. I believe you. Keep in mind that I haven't seen or heard her do or say any of this. So, I'm in the dark. Let's not be those parents, the ones who run to professionals every time they have a behavioral problem. They might want to put her on medication. You don't want that, do you?"

Joseph was right, she didn't want Lily put through a battery of questions or tests followed by prescription drugs. "Yes, you're making sense. Go ahead. See if she will tell you what's bothering her." Holly knew that if anyone could get Lily to open up, it would be her father.

Lily woke up a few minutes later. She stood in her bedroom doorway watching Joseph as he sat rearranging his camera bag. She looked tired and sad. "Hey little lady, did you have a nice nap?" Lily rubbed her eyes, shrugged her shoulders. "How about you come with me down to Jolly's for an ice cream cone?"

She answered with a vigorous nodding of her head and a big smile. Turning to Holly, who still sat on the sofa next to him, he gave her a kiss and winked.

Holly rose and walked toward the kitchen. As she moved beyond Lily's view, she turned and gave Joseph the thumbs up. He nodded.

Lily ambled the few yards to the couch; she plopped down next to Joseph, throwing her arms around his neck.

He would get her out of the house, take her to do something fun, see if he could figure out why she was tormenting her mother. "Put your shoes on and go to the bathroom before we leave. We don't want to have to stop to use the bushes on the way." It was a twenty-four mile stretch from their house to the valley below where a small group of shops formed the closest thing to a town within an hour's drive.

Lily was excited. Not only did she love going places with her daddy, but also, she was crazy about Jolly's. She didn't get to go often for two reasons. One, she was only allowed junk food on rare occasions, and two, Mommy hated the place. She said it gave her the creeps. Lily didn't understand why. To her it was a magical place.

Lily ran for the bathroom. She noticed as she was washing her hands that Mommy's necklace was sitting in the dish next to the sink. That was unusual. Mommy never took it off except to shower and when they went swimming in the summer.

Lily's inner voice tugged at her. "Take it. You might need it." Somewhat begrudgingly, Lily picked up the locket and chain and put it in her pocket. She bounded toward the front door, where she had left her shoes. She slipped them on and fastened the Velcro.

Holly walked them out to the truck and opened the back of the double cab. Lily usually climbed into her booster seat buckling up on her own. Today she asked Holly to help her. Holly was surprised that she didn't ask Joseph. She fastened Lily's buckle and adjusted the strap.

Lily leaned in, whispering in her ear. "This will settle the score." Lily said it without emotion and without understanding. She had no idea what she meant or why she said it.

Holly took a step back. Dumbfounded, she couldn't compose words for either Lily or Joseph. She closed the back door, returning Joseph's hug before he jumped up into his seat, buckled up then pulled out of the driveway.

Alone in the house Holly broke down. She cried and cried until there were no tears left. *What in the name of God had that child meant? Joseph might not be able to fix this. We might need professional help. I might need professional help.* She began to question her sanity. *Should I call the therapist in Tucson that I saw after my accident? I could ask for a referral to someone in this area.* Her head was pounding. She went looking for a pain reliever.

The bathroom cabinet was too low to store medication safely, so they kept it in a high cabinet, in the kitchen. She found the tablets, took two, and then she lay down on the sofa. Soon she was dozing.

Chapter Thirty-Five

Joseph wasted no time in starting a conversation with Lily. He asked her if there were something she wanted to talk about. She said no. He asked about her problems with Holly carefully sidestepping any accusations. Lily's responses were all uninformative.

"I guess you and Mommy had a good time while I was gone."

"Yep."

"You ran away, though, right?"

"We played hide-and-seek."

"Mommy was worried when she couldn't find you. You were gone a long time."

"Mommy isn't very good at that game."

"Did you say mean things to her?"

"Uh-uh."

Joseph wasn't getting anywhere with his line of questioning, so he changed the subject. "What are you going to order at Jolly's?" he teased. He knew it would be a chocolate cherry swirl because she always ordered the same thing.

There were two ways to get to Jolly's. The most direct route took them down Highway 260 and though faster, was actually further mileage-wise. The scenic route, as Joseph called it, was by way of Young Highway, which was mountainous, and mostly unpaved. Joseph took 260.

All the way to Jolly's, Joseph tried to engage Lily in discussion. If he encouraged her to talk, maybe she would say something to give him a clue as to what might be bothering her. She seemed fine to him. She happily talked about her friend Emma, their sleepover, and even chatted about the picnic as though her weekend had been nothing but fun.

Jolly's was hard to miss. The owner, Ms. Dorothy, once worked in a circus; she had a thing for clowns. A giant clown statue graced the entrance. Inside clown paintings, prints, and other images of clowns hung upon a surface of clown print wallpaper.

It was over the top décor. Topping off the exhibition was Dorothy's large collection of clown dolls, which hung about, on shelves above the bright red booths, and above the counter where customers placed their orders. If one had an aversion to clowns, this was not a place to visit. Lily loved it.

They ordered their ice cream, with Lily predictably choosing the chocolate cherry swirl. Lily chose a booth under a clown with orange hair and a huge red nose. Joseph wasn't bothered by the zany jesters staring down from their perches, yet he could understand why Holly was unnerved. She said it reminded her of that novel-turned-TV-movie by Stephen King *It*, about the psychotic clown. For Lily's sake, he was glad she was too young to associate Jolly's with anything sinister.

While they ate, Joseph asked Lily if she was angry with anyone. He thought being vague might be better rather than asking directly if she was mad at her mother. Lily denied being upset or unhappy with anyone. She was giggly and pleasant as always. Joseph began to ponder the idea that maybe Holly was the one he should be talking to.

Lily wasn't about to say anything. She had a trip to Jolly's and ice cream at stake. Besides, she didn't know what to say. If she admitted to Daddy that the voice sometimes made her say ugly words or do bad stuff, he might punish her - or worse, send her away.

When they climbed back into their seats in the truck, Lily asked if they might take the other way home. "I want to stop at the Look-out" Lily loved the view of the canyon.

"I suppose so. Buckle up." Joseph pulled out of Jolly's and headed south-west on 260. When he reached the sign for 288, he would turn left, due south. The sun was getting lower in the sky, creating a glare that challenged Joseph's sunglasses. He hated driving into the sun.

As they traveled along, Joseph became lost in his thoughts. He didn't know what he was going to say to Holly. She would expect him to have resolved the issue with Lily, or at least have a plan. He had nothing.

He could call Cassie; she had known Holly since they were kids. He recalled her warning that Holly had a different personality before the accident. He didn't want to think that his wife was mentally unstable. It had to be a misunderstanding. He would sit down with Holly and Lily. Together they would resolve whatever this was, once and for all.

Lily began singing. It was a song she learned in pre-school. Keeping quiet about the voice brought the song to mind. "If you're quiet and you know it zip your lips." Endlessly she sang. Joseph looked up at the mirror to see her swaying as she sang. She had something in her hand that she was looking at intently.

"What do you have there, Lily?" It was a casual question; at least Joseph meant it as such.

Lily reacted by shoving the object back into her pocket and snapping "Nothing. I didn't do anything."

Joseph wasn't expecting her reaction. Obviously, whatever she had in her pocket was something that she wasn't supposed to have. "Tell me what it is or I'll pull over and check for myself." Now Joseph was flustered. He may have judged Lily all wrong.

In the back seat, Lily started pushing the button to roll down the window. She knew she wasn't supposed to do that. It was dangerous. Even so, opening the window and tossing the necklace out was the only way she could think of to dispose of it before she got in a lot of trouble.

Joseph couldn't believe what he was seeing in the mirror. Lily had never done this before. He used the front controls to roll up her window. She pushed the button again rolling it down slightly. He turned toward her. "Stop it. I can't believe you are going to make me turn on the child safety lock." He gave her a stern look flipping the switch to turn on the security lock.

Joseph made a wide turn onto the narrow two-lane highway that would take them home. Lily knew she didn't have much time to figure out what to do with the locket. She could hide it somewhere in the truck as long as Daddy didn't see her do it. She quietly unfastened her seat belt. She slunk down in her seat, edging herself off the booster. She pulled the necklace from her pocket, holding it tightly in her fist.

Up ahead the road made a snake like curve. On one side, a pullout had been installed for people to get out, look down, and observe the beautiful canyon below. This was where Lily wanted to stop to admire the view.

"We are getting close to the look-out." Lily didn't answer right away because she was on the floor looking for a good hiding place for Mommy's necklace. If she answered, Daddy would know she wasn't in her seat.

He glanced at the mirror. No Lily to be seen. She wasn't in her seat. *Stay calm.* "Lily, honey, you need to get back in your seat now." Suddenly she popped up from behind his seat and grabbed him by the shoulder.

Joseph jumped. He turned toward her, grabbing her by the hand that held fast to the locket. The truck swerved. He felt the tires skid as he braked. He attempted to gain control, but he overcorrected.

The truck began to spin; it hit the guardrail and caught air. Inside the cab, Lily screamed.

Joseph had hit his head. He was out cold. Within seconds, the truck flew down the side of the giant precipice, shorn metal and debris left in its wake.

Then, ominous silence. All was quiet on the mountainside.

Holly woke from her nap, head still aching. Now her mouth felt like the desert. She rose, strolling to the kitchen for a drink. Out the window, the sky was turning all shades of pink. *Joseph and Lily should be home anytime. I should start some dinner.* Something quick would have to do.

She looked through the cabinet for ideas. Tomato soup. Now if there was cheese …. Opening the fridge, she found cheese, bread and butter. *Grilled cheese with soup it is.*

Holly opened the soup can, scooping the contents into a small saucepan. She buttered the bread slices and built the sandwiches. Retrieving a small electric grill from the pantry, she placed it on the counter and plugged it in.

When it was hot enough, she placed the sandwiches on the surface and watched over them, spatula in hand. Outside it was almost dark. The dirt road leading up to their driveway was barely visible. *Where are you?* She was starting to worry.

Headlights turned onto the road. Two sets moving very slowly toward the house. Neither set belonged to Joseph's truck. Holly was sure of that because these lights were too low to the ground. She moved to the picture window in the front room for a better view.

As they approached, she saw that the car in the lead had emergency lights, a sheriff's car. The car in the rear was a dark colored sedan. Holly's heart moved to her throat. It pounded in her ears. She felt dizzy. Her eyes couldn't focus. She heard the doorbell. She walked to the door. Her arm tingled. It felt numb. Holly blacked out. Her body crashed to the floor.

Chapter Thirty-Six

Cassie pulled into the long drive leading up to the Shady Lane Convalescent Home. It was a depressing drive that she had made monthly since Holly had been admitted to the home two years ago.

After the stroke she suffered in the wake of Joseph's and Lily's deaths, Holly spent time in the hospital, followed by weeks in the rehab center. Finally, when the doctors ran out of ideas, she had been moved to this center, where those with no hope of returning to their previous lives were housed. Thank goodness the staff was polite and caring, for the general atmosphere of the place was dark and gloomy.

The buildings of the center were once the site of a mental hospital; the interior, though now painted in cheery colors, still had an institutional feel. The rooms were small with large, heavy metal doors.

Narrow hallways and high ceilings created echoes that amplified the sound of carts being pushed, trays being passed, and patients crying out. The air was thick with deodorizer working hard to cover odors that refused to be quelled.

Cassie hated the place, yet Holly needed her, needed somebody. She was alone in the world, though she might not be cognizant enough to realize it.

Entering the sterile room that was Holly's home, if you could call it that, Cassie felt claustrophobic. The blinds were closed, the curtains were drawn, and only one lamp with a dim bulb lit the small space. Holly was at least out of bed, which was a plus. The shell that was once Cassie's best friend sat in a wheelchair, eyes glazed, staring.

Stroke induced catatonia. Her left side paralyzed and drooping, she slumped to one side. Every day a new set of symptoms seemed to manifest. Some days she would repeat motions in tic-like fashion for hours. Other days she held rigid poses for extensive periods.

Her speech was slurred and meaningless. Occasionally she would repeat a word that someone said to her, unceasingly until fatigue finally halted the repetition.

Cassie wondered if Holly even knew of her visits. Her eyes welled up with tears. She thought about what it must be like to be trapped in there, in a body that could no longer function. Holly would not want to live like this if she were able to choose. Powerless to help her, Cassie did all she could do. She just kept showing up. Stomping toward the window, she flung the drapes aside, pulling open the blinds letting the fading sunlight into the room. She heaved a huge sigh.

"Would it be too much to ask that these people open the damned curtains? Maybe even crack a window to let in some fresh air?"

Cassie had to keep busy during these visits, even if it meant barging around, complaining, fussing with the furnishings. She tidied the bed and straightened the few items on top of Holly's dresser. A comb, brush, and an outdated magazine, probably left there by one of the nurses because Holly wasn't likely to be thumbing through the pages of *Glamour* any time soon.

Rules indicated that any toiletries that might be pilfered by and possibly consumed by wandering patients, such as shampoo, lotion, and toothpaste must be kept under lock and key. It was a spartan life.

Holly was making little sounds like the chirping of a bird. Cassie walked to her. Bending-over, she kissed her forehead. "I'm going to go ascertain what can be done to lighten up this room, make it more cheerful. I'll be back in a few minutes."

She bustled down the hallway past patients sitting lost in their own worlds. If she were lucky, there would be someone with a little authority in the office at the front of the building.

The Trine manifested in the corner of Holly's room in much the same way as they had in Emeline's 'locket' room. Holly could see them. Her eyes opened wide with shock.

Raya spoke first, "She is being given a rare opportunity."

"Can she move on, this time?" Aya wanted to know.

"The question is not can she, but will she," Raya explained. "Emeline is no different from any mortal soul. Most move on when the time comes, because the light takes away their fear. Fear of death, fear of loss, fear of the unknown. Some souls hold back. They never let the light take that fear away."

Maya nodded in agreement. "It is a shame. Still, there is nothing we can do. We can only show them the road. They will go where they choose."

Aya removed an item from her cloak. Approaching Holly, she placed the item in Holly's hand.

In unison, they said "Look into the glass, and whom do you see? Is it the one you wish to be? Awaken now and see the past. Your choice now could be your last." Holly looked at the mirror. Slowly it slid off her lap and onto the tile floor.

Emeline spontaneously emerged from the heavy mist which surrounded her while she lived in the fugue state of catatonia. She tried to speak, to move her limbs to no avail. It seemed that only her mind was now back to normal.

No, "normal" was not the correct word for the thought processes she now received like a tidal wave. She could see everything now, everything that was hers to see.

The many lifetimes she lived with Jonathan or Joseph, who held many names over many centuries. Their child, who had always been a girl.

She saw that there were no villains in the length of their story for each of them was guilty of the human vices: Jealousy, betrayal, guilt, remorse, and pride, among others.

Now that she had been given this gift to see the pattern, it was up to her to break the cycle. This material world was something she had to let go of in order to move on.

It wouldn't be hard to do now that her family had gone before her, although this was where she last found herself resisting, holding back, latching on to the locket. That locket was gone now. She wanted to reach up and rip it off. A ball and chain, that was what it had been. Her body, the one she had essentially stolen was failing her. She took one last breath.

She found herself free, floating in the tunnel that she and Holly had used to escape from the locket. The Trine stood at the end of the long tunnel waiting beside the gigantic door. She went toward them.

As she moved closer, she heard the tune far off in the distance echoing throughout the hallway. The lullaby once again. *He must be here. He's waited for me.* She continued toward the women. Their arms were outstretched, they beckoned with their eyes as if they were willing her onward.

The song was closer now, just behind her. Emeline drew in a familiar scent. Men's cologne. She began to turn her head. Out of the corner of her eye, she saw the Trine reaching out, they were now only a few feet away. Deep within, her old feelings and worries swelled. Her love of lifetimes was there in the tunnel. Emeline wondered what would happen to him if she left him behind. He would follow her, she was sure of it.

It was decision time. Emeline propelled herself forward. Her being was now pure energy, an opalescent ball of light. Aya moved to the door and pulled it open by the large brass handle. Beyond that portal, all would be made new.

"Slower and slower and slower the wheel rings. Lower and lower and lower the reel rings. E're the reel and the wheel stopped their ringing and moving, through the grove the young lovers by moonlight are roving."

It was as if she could feel his breath on her neck as he sang the words. *Jonathan, Joseph ...* She slowed. She turned.

She woke slowly, bit by bit. Aware that she was in a bodily form, still she knew what it felt like to be pure Spirit. Unsure as to who she was, let alone where she was, she gradually opened her eyes.

Joseph noticed her stirring and came to her side. "Thank goodness, I'm glad you're awake. Can I bring you anything?"

She looked around. She lay on the couch in their front room, she could see the entrance to the kitchen and the front door. Everything seemed just as it had the last time she had been there. *Just when was that?* Things, thoughts were fuzzy.

Holly swiveled to look outside through the picture window. The window was gone. In its place was a large oval ornate antique mirror. She recognized it. A gasp escaped her throat.

Again. But I couldn't be back inside the locket. I haven't seen it since before Joseph and Lily died. It's okay, no matter where we are, this time I have my family here with me. We are together, finally.

She turned to look behind her. There was the small hallway that led to the bedrooms. Lily's door was closed.

"Where's Lily?" Concern crept into her consciousness.

"Lily moved on as she should have. We will find her again, or she will find us. I'm sure of it." Joseph sounded calm, resolved.

Holly's eyes brimmed with tears. "I know you are right. We do seem to always find each other." Joseph handed Holly a tissue from a box on the coffee table. She wiped her eyes. Then she rose from the couch feeling better than she had in a long time. She and Joseph embraced. They shared a long, deep kiss. She was home.

Epilogue

20 years later

The young woman steered her car into the pullout marked Scenic Lookout. She couldn't wait any longer. Her bladder felt as though it might explode.

This stretch of highway, a shortcut her friend had said, seemed to go on forever with no facilities to speak of. Her two-week spring break was almost over. During that time, she had driven a lot of miles, visiting college campuses in New Mexico and Arizona. She hoped to transfer to one of them in the fall.

The southwest called to her, though she had never been to this part of the country before. *Maybe growing up in the south filled me with a desire to dry out for a change.*

She parked the car and wandered over to the edge of the deep canyon. A railing about three feet high provided some sense of safety; even so, the height made her feel woozy. She looked around at the landscape. Junipers, pines, and aspens lined the roadway. If she shimmied down the embankment nearest her parked car, she could relieve herself behind a tree without being seen by passing vehicles.

She was glad she had on her hiking boots and an old pair of jeans. Grabbing tissues and wet wipes from her glove box, she headed for the trees. As she reached the largest of the pines and squatted down next to it, she saw some debris lodged in the lower branches.

Finished with the business at hand, she inspected the contents of the branches. Some old papers with faded pages, some worn fabric that might have once been clothing, and lastly, a chain with an old worn brass colored locket charm attached. Crusted and old, the hinges, stuck in place, it was just a piece of junk.

She started to leave it where she found it… *wait, maybe it's an antique. It might be worth something.* She shook the dirt off of the old necklace, and put it in her pocket.

www.ingramcontent.com/pod-product-compliance
Lightning Source LLC
Chambersburg PA
CBHW020325260626
47156CB00004B/1379